Sweet Little Thing

a novella

RENÉE CARLINO

Table of Contents

For the readers, the lovers, and the dreamers.

TRACK 1: Wedding Pains

"Tyler is getting ordained online as we speak," I said to Mia as I watched her anxiously thumb through a bridal magazine. She was sitting in the window ledge of our Brooklyn loft, wearing an oversized wool sweater and bright purple leggings. Her hair was knotted up on the top of her head in a messy bun. I was sitting at the breakfast bar across the room, slurping up a bowl of cereal.

"Tyler is going to marry us?"

"Yeah, why not? Who better than my best friend?"

"I can think of a few people, like Martha or Sheil."

"Tyler will be perfect!"

She stared me down for several seconds and then very subtly shook her head.

I wouldn't go as far as to say that Mia was getting cold feet about marrying me, but she definitely wasn't into planning the wedding. We'd decided the day Mia moved to Brooklyn that we wouldn't waste another minute. We would head down to the courthouse, pick up a witness off the street, get hitched, and call it a day. That was until

Jenny caught wind of our little plan, God love her. I say that with the utmost love, respect, and pure sarcasm. Jenny threw a wrench in the whole freakin' plan. As soon as she'd found out, she'd immediately called Mia's mom and blabbered everything to her. Jenny was like that. A good friend, but man, once in a while she overstepped the boundaries.

Of course Mia's mom put a guilt trip on both of us. I can't tell you how many times I heard her over the speakerphone: "But you're my only child, Mia, and I'm not invited to your wedding?" Liz could be melodramatic at times, even though she was a pretty grounded human being in general. It wasn't that we didn't want her at our wedding, it was that we didn't feel we needed a wedding to begin with. And it wasn't Mia who eventually gave in—no, my little firecracker stuck to her guns. I'm the wuss who rolled over.

All Mia's step-dad had to say to me was, "Gee, Will, I sure hope your future daughters let you walk them down the aisle." Aw, man, that went straight to my gut. I got gut punched by a hypothetical situation. Who knew if we would even have a daughter, much less one who didn't want me to walk her down the aisle? Yet that's all it took; just the mere thought of not being present at my future kid's wedding was enough for me to call off the instant nuptials.

Mia was mad at me for a week until we had really great make-up sex, and then she got over it. That's when the bridal magazines starting popping up everywhere. I'm pretty sure that was Jenny's sneaky little touch, but even with all the wedding propaganda flashing in front of Mia's face, I could tell she wasn't buying into it.

Sitting on the ledge and staring out the window, she said, "What does your dream wedding look like, Will?"

I looked up to the ceiling and scratched my chin. I knew I could say something really romantic in that moment, but I loved messing with Mia. "Hmm?" I waited for her to finally turn her head and look at me. "Remember the video for 'November Rain'? Guns N' Roses?" I wiggled my eyebrows at her.

She scrunched up her nose and squinted but then burst into a fit of laughter. She laughed so hard she fell off the ledge and cried and then made a hilarious attempt at speaking. "Your dream, bahahaha. Your dream is to marry a six-foot-tall supermodel while you sit at a piano wearing a bandana?" She tried to catch her breath and then her eyes shot open even wider. "You know that dream doesn't end well? Doesn't the bride die?" Her voice got really high.

I managed to remain deadpan even though I wanted to laugh and roll around on the ground with her. Instead, I pretended she'd hurt my feelings. "We could probably get Slash to shred on his guitar in the dusty wind outside the church," I said, looking doe-eyed at her.

Her face went completely blank as she lay on the ground staring up at me. "You are not serious. Since when were you such a butt-rocker? Did you like that hair-band shit?"

"I'm older than you, Mia. That was kind of my time."

"Please tell me you didn't have bangs."

I stalked over to the old upright and began playing "November Rain." I belted out the lines in my best scratchy-voiced, Axl Rose impression.

Mia crept up behind me and wrapped her arms around my waist, pressing her cheek to my back. "Please stop, honey, please?"

I plopped down on the piano bench and turned, pulling her onto my lap. I kissed her shoulder and then her neck. She shivered.

"It doesn't matter to me what our wedding looks like as long as you're there."

"Wearing white?"

Between kisses, I said, "You can wear whatever you want. You can wear a trash bag for all I care. I'll still want to marry you and kiss you like this for the rest of my life."

She cupped my face. "Wilbur, you are so sexy when you're not pretending to be an eighties butt-rocker."

"You know what's not sexy?"

"What?" she said on a breath between laying kisses on my cheek.

"June pooping on the floor."

Mia jumped off my lap and darted over to the kitchen, screeching in her highest voice. "No, no, no, Juney." She caught our little puppy mid-poop and picked her up, held her arms out and screamed, "What do I do?"

There was no way Mia would be able to get June outside without leaving a trail of poop in her wake. "Put her over the toilet!"

I followed her as she ran down the hallway and into our tiny bathroom at the end. She held the squirming puppy over the toilet until the doggie business was complete.

Setting June on the ground, she glanced up at me,

frowned, and then mumbled, "I'm gonna be a terrible mother."

I helped her up and then stood behind her at the sink as she washed her hands. "No, you're going to be perfect." I smirked when she looked at me in the mirror. "You did exactly the right thing. First you screamed and charged at her with your arms flailing around, and then you basically held her by the neck while you ran around in a circle yelling. That is exactly what you will probably do if the same situation happens to play out with one of our babies."

"Thanks a lot."

"I'm kidding." I pinched her butt.

"Ouch, jerk-face!"

"Baby, look at me." Once she turned, I continued. "You are good at everything you do. Trust me... everything." I let my eyes drop to her mouth.

"Oh, stop." She tried to squirm out of my embrace.

"No, seriously, Mia. You're gonna be a great mom." I squeezed her tighter when she huffed into my chest. "I have to get down to the studio; that tool, Chad, and his people scheduled a jam session. Whatever the fuck that means when you don't play any instruments."

"I'll be down in a little bit," she said. "Hey, why do you think they came to us? Chad and his people?" She held up air quotes when she said the word "people." "It doesn't really seem like a good fit."

"You're right, but the record label said we'll basically write all his songs, play every instrument on the album, and then pretty boy can sit at the front of the stage playing air guitar and pretending he's a musician. It's Milli Vanilli shit."

"What label?" she asked.

"Live Wire."

She sucked in a breath. Live Wire was the label that had basically tried to make me their monkey back when I was looking for a record deal. I'd signed with them but hadn't been able to deliver the bubblegum-pop shit they wanted. When I tried to get out of the contract, they sued me. Luckily, Frank had scrutinized the deal so carefully he was able to find a mistake on their end, which basically revoked the entire deal. I'd gone on and opened Alchemy Sound Studios, but remained cautious when it came to working with the labels.

"You're not going to let them take credit for your songs, are you?"

"Our songs, and of course not. Frank is handling the contract on this one because they came to me with no material. A good-looking kid with a decent voice who's willing to do anything comes along and bam, record deal, no songs required. He doesn't care if the label makes him sing 'You're My Fucking Sunshine,' all he cares about is screaming girls. We'll get writing and producing credits on it, and we'll get paid well. Frank will work it out so we don't get screwed. I promise, baby."

Frank Abedo was the talent agent who'd gotten me signed with Live Wire. He believed in me and thought I had a rare talent. He genuinely wanted the business to be about the music, so he'd understood when I'd wanted to get out of my contract. After I opened Alchemy Sound Studios, he stuck around, even though there was nothing in it for him. He brought a lot of talent my way, and he was well-versed when it came to contracts, so he was definitely an asset for our team.

When I got down to the studio, Chad was waiting in the lobby with his manager.

"Thanks for waiting, guys. Follow me."

I'd hired another producer and an assistant just out of college. Both guys were already in the control room setting up the sound board.

"Let's record everything today," I announced. "We need to get some layers down."

Chad followed me into the room beyond the glass where all the instruments were sitting. I picked up my acoustic guitar, took a seat, and motioned for Chad to sit in the chair near the vocal mic. I noticed he had a notebook under his arm. Chad was the darker-haired version of Zac Efron; he even had the adorable, chummy smile and glowing blue eyes.

"Whaddya got, bro?" I said to him, dipping my head toward his arm.

He looked nervous. "Oh, these are just some lyrics I wrote. Hey, by the way, I'm totally stoked to be working with you."

"Thanks. You know, typically we get the music down first, but let me take a look."

He handed it over and then crossed his arms and sat back in his chair.

I read the first line: *Girl, you're my girl.*

I immediately shut the notebook, tossed it aside, and said, "We'll revisit that later."

"Oh, okay, no problem."

I played a few rough versions of songs while Chad sat by, looking lost. Mia came in wearing black leather pants and a tight sweater. As I strummed the Gibson, she made her way over to the piano. She smiled and threw her hand up, waving to Chad. He smiled back and then I watched him study her as she passed. Then his dipshit, googly eyes dropped to her ass while she moved the piano bench out.

When he looked back at me, I glared at him and began strumming a dreary and much louder tune. His body sank into his chair and he dropped his head down to stare at his fidgeting hands. Mia began playing a sullen little melody in an attempt to accompany the monotonous song I was forming, and then she stopped abruptly and turned toward me.

I continued playing.

"Is this going to be a ballad?" she asked.

Without taking my eyes off of dipshit, I said, "No, baby, this is what's called a funeral march."

Chad threw his arms up and said, "I get it. I get it. I'm sorry."

"Sorry for what?" Mia asked.

"Nothing!" Chad and I both shouted.

"Let's move on," I said, arching one eyebrow at him.

Chad kept his eyes trained on either the ground or me through the rest of the session. He never once looked back at Mia. We managed to get down rough versions of four songs. There was one gorgeous ballad that Mia composed on the piano that had Chad's manager doing backflips. It was heartbreaking to think such a beautiful song, written with passion and depth by a beautiful person, was going to be performed by some dweeby kid, but that's the other side of the coin, I guess.

Mia and I had made a decision that this was what we

wanted. I'd passed on my opportunity for commercial success as a recording artist. It had been one of the toughest decisions of my life. Mia had never strived for that sort of fame; she knew it came with a price. Instead, we'd found a way to still make music but maintain normalcy. The only thing that sucked was that we had to give our songs to other people, people like Chad.

Later that night, back in our apartment, Mia came skipping into our bedroom. "All right, I've got an idea. I think we should have everyone meet us on the Fulton Ferry Landing at one o'clock. We'll write super simple vows. Tyler can say whatever garbage he needs to say, then we'll kiss and be married and everyone will be happy."

Sitting against the wooden headboard, I propped my hands behind my head. "Gosh, that is so romantic, Mia."

"What?" she whined.

"You know there are at least five weddings happening on the Fulton Ferry Landing every Saturday?"

"The more the merrier!" she said with a cheesy grin.

"You know what, I take it back. You're right. We don't have to have a wedding. Christ, do you know how much it would cost to feed every member of my family? Whoever wants to come, can come out. We'll do the vows like you said, at the ferry landing, take some pictures, go to dinner, and then catch the first flight out of here and go to the Bahamas and blow our money there."

"That's a perfect idea."

"Okay, you deal with your mom, Martha, and Sheil, and I'll deal with Jenny and Tyler. Jenny's going to be pissed; she was looking into permits to have a fireworks show."

We both laughed.

Mia said, "It's funny how Jenny didn't want a big wedding but thinks everyone else should have one. Oh, I wanted to ask you. What kind of ring do you think you would like?"

I hadn't thought once about my wedding ring. "Should we get tats?"

"You want me to get a tattoo?"

"Yeah, why not?"

"Okay." She flashed me a small, tight smile and then began gnawing on her nails.

"Are you scared of the needle?"

"No." She watched me as I processed her reaction.

"Do you like my tattoos?"

"Yeah, I love them," she said passionately, and then it hit me.

"Oh, baby, I love your skin too. I love that virgin skin, and I'm not letting anyone ink it."

"Okay, thanks." She chewed off a hefty piece of her thumbnail. Mia hated her hands and nails. Because she played the piano with so much fervor and for many years, her hands were bulky compared to the rest of her petite features. She would gnaw on her nails because she hated the way they looked, and I think it calmed her nerves too.

"Jesus, lady, go easy. Your thumb is bleeding." She looked down at it and shrugged. "By the way, I have a bone to pick with you." I said.

"I despise that saying on so many levels."

"Why?"

"Think about it. Picking bones, that's disgusting." She said, scrunching her nose up.

"I could make that argument about chewing on your thumbs, but I'll let it go. I have a complaint."

She climbed up next to me and cuddled her face up to my bare chest, then she used her index finger to trace a line down my happy trail to the belt on my jeans.

"What sort of complaint, Wilbur?" *Ah, Mia's sexy voice.*

I reached down and ran my hand up her thigh. "You should not wear these pants around that horny little *High School Musical* kid."

She popped up and looked me straight in the face. "He totally looks like Zac Efron, huh?"

"Mia, he practically shot off a load just staring at your ass."

She punched me in the chest. "That is vulgar, Will Ryan."

"It's true. You can't dress like that around him." I tackled her back down on the bed and hovered over her.

"I thought you liked these pants."

"I do." I began kissing my way down her body. I lifted her shirt and kissed the swell of each breast before moving down the center of her body. "But you know what I like better than you in these pants?"

"Me out of these pants?"

"Am I that predictable?" I said as I quickly peeled them off her body.

"Yes." She sighed.

I sat back on my heels. "You're beautiful."

Holding her leg from behind her knee, I kissed my way up the inside, from her calf to her thigh and all the way up to her panties. I peeled the lace from her hips with my teeth and then down to her ankles as slowly as possible. She lay there naked from the waist down, watching me gaze at her, hungry for her. Her skin was pure white and it contrasted so strikingly against her dark eyes and hair. She was an authentic beauty. I leaned over her body, putting my weight on my hands, which were placed on each side of her head. Her eyes were searching mine. She whimpered and then tried to lift her face up to kiss me.

I drew my head back. "Uh uh, I don't think so." I nuzzled my nose into her neck and trailed kisses to her ear. I whispered, "Stay just like this. Don't go anywhere." I planted a swift kiss on her lips and jumped off the bed. "I'm goin' to play B-ball with Tyler. Be back in a few."

As I left the room, I glanced over my shoulder and saw her lying there completely still, her mouth open in shock. I got halfway down the hallway before she finally yelled, "Asshole!"

I bent in the hallway and patted June's head. She rolled over and then got back on her feet and trotted off toward our bedroom.

Before walking out the door, I called back to Mia, "Who's predictable now, sweet thing?"

TRACK 2: The Creation Process

I n the weeks following our introduction to Chad, we were able to get eight solid songs laid down for his album. He had a decent voice, likely attributable to the well-paid vocal coach Live Wire had hired. There wasn't much I could do about the fact that he sounded so young. I wished for more depth behind the vocals, but Chad wasn't physically mature or trained enough to control his voice in that way. Once we were comfortable with the music, Mia skipped most of the sessions. She liked to be a part of the creation process but often got frustrated during the long post-production sessions, so she would let the other producers and me handle that.

During one session, Chad's manager, Michael Dolan, came to me with a concern. He was a pretty straight-laced guy from what I could tell. Chad's parents looked to Michael as a manager but also as a babysitter for the nineteen-year-old budding superstar. Their concern was that once Chad tasted a moderate amount of fame, he would instantly become the male version of Lindsay

Lohan. I didn't see that in Chad. He was too naïve; at least, I thought he was. I really believed Chad was the puppet. I'd thought if we ever ran into a problem, it would be with the label, so it was to my absolute shock and horror when Michael came to me and said, "Chad wants to be in on all the sessions. He doesn't feel like he's getting enough creative control on the songs he's written." Michael was hovering over me as I sat at the sound board, shocked.

I swiveled my chair around to make eye contact and noticed that Chad was cowering behind him. I leaned my head around, looked Chad right in the face, and said, "What fucking songs, Mike?"

Michael took a step sideways to block the eye lasers I was shooting at Chad. "Now, Will, no need to lose your temper."

"I totally agree. Why don't we start with the songs that Chad thinks he's written?"

"To begin with, 'Lost N Found,'" Michael said.

I jumped out of my seat. "You mean the piano ballad that Mia composed, the very song you watched her write?"

"I wouldn't say that Mia wrote that song."

"You're saying that he wrote it?" I shot my index finger out in Chad's direction.

"Yes."

"Okay." I clapped my hands once, reached around Michael, and grabbed pansy-ass Chad by the ear and proceeded to drag him from the control room to the sound room.

"Ouch," he said and tried to pull away.

"Oh, I'm sorry. Does that hurt?"

"Whoa, whoa, whoa, Will. This is assault." Michael

was shouting behind us.

I was fuming mad. I stopped and turned toward Chad. "You know what hurts? Wasting my time trying to help a little fuck-nut like you. Let's go." I pulled him over to the piano and pushed him down on the bench. "Okay. Play your song, Chad."

He looked up at Michael like a deer in headlights.

Michael said, "Wait a minute, Will."

"Shut up, Mike." I turned back to Chad. "Okay, fine. I know you can't play the super-complicated masterpiece that my sweet, darling Mia wrote and was willing to *let you perform*!" I shouted. "Instead, why don't you just play us 'Mary Had a Little Lamb'? Go ahead. Show us your musical prowess, Chaddy Boy. How about you start on the E above middle C?"

He didn't even put his hands on the keys; he just stared up at Michael and me and waited for someone to rescue him. My phone buzzed in my pocket. I pulled it out and read a text from Mia: **I'll be at Kell's until 5. Do u wanna stay in 2nite and have naked dinner?**

I didn't answer. Instead, I put the phone back in my pocket and took a deep breath. It was like Mia could sense when I needed her. There was this invisible string connecting our souls and it was as though we could feel each other tug on that string when we were hurting. I calmed significantly after reading her text.

I looked down and in a relaxed, smooth voice I said, "Chad, do you know where middle C is?"

He shook his head very slowly.

I looked up to Michael. "The contract is void. I'll deal with Live Wire." I picked up Chad's notebook from the top of the piano and handed it to him. "Take your songs and get the fuck out of my studio."

Chad mumbled something as he walked toward the door, to which Michael replied, "It's okay." Then he turned to me and said, "You'll be hearing from our lawyer."

I said nothing in response. Staring out the front window, I watched until their car was out of sight. There was no one else in the studio that day, so I very solemnly closed up and rode the subway into the village. I stood outside of Kell's, the coffee shop Mia had inherited after her father died. There was something warm about that place, like it held the type of familiarity a childhood home does. It was dusk and from the outside looking in, the café's warm lighting was inviting; it always felt like a safe place. I know Mia felt that way too. I swung the door open and was immediately greeted by Martha.

"Will, what a pleasure, honey." She came up to me and kissed both of my cheeks. Martha was a longtime friend to Mia's father. After he died, she'd remained a very big and influential part of Mia's life. She also, along with Jenny, ran the coffee shop so that Mia could focus on music and getting the studio going. Still, Mia spent a lot of time with Martha at the café. I looked past the old, shining espresso machine that everyone called the monster and searched the rest of room but didn't see Mia.

"Hi, Martha. Is Mia in the back?"

"No, she ran to the store and then she was going to drop by Jenny's for a minute. She should be back soon. Have a seat—I'll make you a cappuccino."

Jenny and Tyler, who were basically our best friends, had moved into the apartment Mia and I use to share on the same street as the café. Mia had also inherited the building, so she was basically renting the apartment out to Jenny and Tyler for dirt cheap. I didn't care. Mia had a huge heart and I loved that she took care of the people who loved her.

I sat at the bar facing out the front window and sipped my coffee. I watched a piece of paper float and twirl and fly up and fall down, all at the mercy of the wind.

Martha stood behind me and watched the paper as well, until finally the wind carried it into the street where it was violently hit and pushed away by a passing car.

"Sometimes we're just along for the ride," she said over my shoulder. "We can't control everything; we can only do our best to control our reactions when life doesn't go our way."

I spun the barstool around to look at her. "What do you mean?"

"Oh, nothing," she said before turning on her heel and heading back to the counter.

I whirled back around to look out the window again and immediately spotted Mia. She was across the street and down a little way, standing underneath the bright fluorescent lights of the corner market. She had a paper bag in one hand and June's leash in the other. It was dusk and starting to get cold. Mia zipped up her jacket and adjusted the bag under her arm. June was hopping all over the place like a maniac. Mia tried unsuccessfully for several minutes to get her to walk in a straight line. As I watched her, I thought how different it was to see her from afar as opposed to when she was in my arms. The kind of beauty that Mia possessed cannot be locked away. It cannot be kept, it's not for me to own and steal away from the world. That realization suddenly gave me a new outlook on getting married.

Marrying her was not for me to claim her as mine. Marriage is about the other person. I thought about that for a long time, watching as she slowly made her way down the street with June in tow. By marrying her, I would be promising to let Mia grow more fully into herself and become even more beautiful while I sat by watching, only getting involved when she tugged on those invisible strings connecting our souls. Mia would not be my wife to fulfill some need or occupy a void. Calling her my wife just meant that I would always get a front-row seat to her beauty as long as I cherished and respected it.

That's why I stayed on the stool that day, just watching. True love is the ironically selfless need to know that your person will be okay without you.

She walked down and crossed the street near our old apartment where Jenny and Tyler currently lived. At one point, June pulled in the opposite direction, and instead of yanking on her leash, Mia just bent and scooped her up. When she disappeared into the building, I put my head down on the bar, closed my eyes, and starting humming the song I had written for her over a year before, when I didn't think I would ever get to be in the front row.

My phone buzzed. I looked down to another text from Mia: **Not in the mood for naked dinner?**

I had forgotten that I hadn't responded and sent back: **I'm always in the mood for naked dinner.**

I'm at Jenny's now. Gonna head home in a few minutes.

I'm at Kell's. I'll wait for you.

It was only about ten minutes before I saw Mia walking hurriedly past the big glass windows to the café door. She was wearing a black peacoat that fell past her knees. Half her face was bundled behind a layered gray scarf. She stalked right up to me as she pulled the scarf off and threw it on the wooden bar. I swiveled toward her so she could stand between my legs, and she put her hands on my face and kissed me quickly, as if to check if I was breathing.

"What's wrong, baby?" she asked. "Why are you here?"

God, I love her. "Do you think everyone in love feels the way we do?"

She laughed once through her nose and hugged me to her chest. "We are so lucky, aren't we?"

"I had a horrible day."

She leaned back to look at my face. "What happened?"

"Uh, well, Chad and Michael came in and claimed that Chad wrote your ballad. They said Chad should have more creative control. What a crock of shit, huh?"

"Oh my God. What assholes. You know what, Will? You should have told them to have at it. Chad can't even play an instrument. I doubt he knows what to do with his own dick, let alone a thirty-two-track sound board."

"I just told them to get out. I'll let Frank deal with Live Wire."

"Will, we signed a contract."

"Fuck the contract."

She took a deep breath and then I watched as she began to tear up.

"Oh, Jesus, Mia, what are you so worried about?"

"We just need stability. We're starting a life together."

A tear escaped and ran down her cheek. I brushed it away with my thumb.

"Everything will be fine," I whispered. "You trust me, right?"

She nodded.

"What was in the bag you took to Jenny's?"

She swallowed hard. "A pregnancy test."

"Oh, man. I hope it was positive; they've been trying for so long."

Jenny had had a miscarriage earlier that year and afterward she and Tyler had tried without success for several months to get pregnant.

"Yeah," Mia said, staring out the window. "I left June at Jenny's. I need to go get her and then we can head home."

When I stood up, I looked over to Martha at the counter. She was standing with her hand on her hip, giving Mia a disapproving look.

"What?" Mia said to her.

Martha huffed. "Where's my hug?"

We both laughed as we walked toward her.

She hugged us at the same time for longer than usual and then said, "You have all you need right here between the two of you."

As we walked out of the café, I said to Mia, "What do you think she meant?"

Mia shrugged and said, "Who knows?"

Back at our loft in Brooklyn, Mia made dinner while wearing nothing but a frilly apron. It covered most of the front of her body but left her backside completely exposed.

I loved that Mia was unaware of what her body did to me or to anyone, for that matter. She didn't prance around sexily, but she wasn't insecure either. She was just comfortable in her skin.

She set a steaming bowl of mushroom risotto in front of me as I sat quietly at the counter. "Why are you so quiet, Will? More importantly, why are you still dressed? This is not fair."

"I'm just thinking about the bullshit that went down with Chad."

"That's what you're thinking about right now?" She turned toward the stove and glanced back at her naked backside before giving me a displeased look.

"I'm also admiring the view." I smirked.

She strutted back to me and pulled my bowl away just as I was about to reach for the fork. "You said it yourself, everything will be fine. Now go get naked or no dinner for you."

I came back out wearing boxers. Mia had moved dinner to our small square table near the edge of the kitchen. We normally sat at the bar to eat unless we were having a more formal dinner. I sat down at the table. Mia came over and set her bowl right next to mine, then took a seat on my lap.

"Mm. Good choice," I whispered behind her ear and then took in the crisp, clean scent of her hair.

"I thought you would like it." She leaned over and began eating.

I sat back and ran my hands up and down her bare sides, all the way up to where the sides of her breasts were peeking from the apron and back down to her hips. I gripped her hard and pulled her back so that her ass was more flush against me. She moaned and then set down her fork.

"We'll starve to death if we keep up this naked dinner tradition."

"I don't care." She stood up but kept her back to me. "Take off your boxers."

My hands moved so fast that my boxers were a blur as I flung them into the other room. I sat back on the chair as she slowly lowered herself onto me, never turning around to see my expression. She probably knew it would resemble something like ecstasy.

She whimpered and then quickly sucked in a breath through her teeth. At first the friction was more intense in that position.

"Does it hurt, baby?"

"No, I just have to get used to it." She moved slowly and very gently up and down, and then after a minute, I could tell she became more comfortable as she started moving in small circles.

I undid the knot of her apron, pulled it over her head, and tossed it aside as she continued grinding on top of me. I ran my hands up and down the soft skin at her sides and then to the front, where I cupped her breasts and pulled her harder so that her back was against my chest. She cried out but didn't let up on her movements. Her breathing became rapid along with mine. I moved my hand down her front, between her breasts, and past her stomach until my fingers reached the place where our bodies joined. I touched her and moved my hand with the rhythm.

"No, stop!" she cried out. Reaching for my hand, she tried to pull it away but she didn't stop writhing on top of me. Her back was arched but her head was thrown all the way back and resting on my shoulder as she whimpered and breathed with her eyes focused on the ceiling.

I licked and sucked at her neck. "You're so close," I said as I started to let her pull my hand away.

The moment my fingers lost contact with her body, she slammed my hand back down. "Don't stop," she said and then cried out, "Oh, God!" before breaking into a boneless fit of spasms.

She lay back on me, her body convulsing as I gripped her and felt my own release. I nuzzled my face into her neck and shoulder and just waited until our breaths returned to normal.

"I'm sure the risotto is cold," she murmured.

"I've never cared less about anything in my life," I said as I lifted her off me to stand.

She turned and reached up on her toes and then threw her arms around my neck.

"Let's go take a shower. I'll heat up dinner afterward."

Lying in bed that night, something peculiar happened. Weeks prior, Mia had convinced me that we should crate train June. That meant putting her in a little cage at night so she wouldn't chew things and poop all over our loft. We'd spent several miserable nights listening to her yelp from the cage, but Mia kept saying, "This will work, trust me. We did it with Jackson. June will eventually love it in there."

I would beg Mia, "Please, I can't take this torture; let's let her out."

Mia would always say, "No. Come on, we have to be a team."

That one peculiar night as we lay there in the dark, staring up at the ceiling and waiting for June to begin her torturous song, something changed in Mia. June only let out just the tiniest yelp, and Mia very slowly got up, walked to the cage, picked June up and said, "It's okay, baby girl," to her as she patted her on the head. She set June between us and slid back into bed.

I let June curl up on my pillow, literally on top of my head, and then I turned to Mia. "Hey, my little ball-buster, are you getting soft on me?" I said to her.

"No." She sighed. "I just need to get some sleep."

"What happened to teamwork?"

"Choosing my battles," she said groggily before dozing off.

TRACK 3: The Fuckin' Hollies

T yler and I were sitting in a shit-hole bar in Brooklyn, having a midday beer and talking about profound things like why some sports teams, like the Florida Marlins, are assigned to states and others, like the Boston Red Sox, belong to cities.

"I've often pondered the very same question," Tyler said.

"It's why I don't watch sports. Nothing makes sense and it's a pointless pastime. If you're the athlete competing, it's one thing, but to just sit there and watch? What's the point? We don't sit around watching people paint pictures."

"That would be extremely boring, Will."

"Are you telling me that baseball isn't boring? I used to get bored playing it as a kid."

Distracted, Tyler looked up to the ceiling. "What's this song called?"

That bar always played the most recognizable classic rock songs. "It's 'Long Cool Woman in a Black Dress.'"

"Oh, man, my dad used to love CCR," he blabbered.

"This isn't Creedence Clearwater Revival, bro, it's the Hollies."

"You're full of shit. My dad would play these guys nonstop. Anyway, who else sounds like this?"

"The fuckin' Hollies do, I'm telling you." I opened my eyes really big for emphasis.

"You don't know everything about music, Will. I know you think you do. This is CCR. I'd bet money on it."

"Okay, fine. If you're right, which you're not, I'll buy everyone in this bar a drink. If I'm right, all you have to do is buy me a drink."

"Deal," he said, but before he Googled it on his phone, he stood up and made an announcement. "This genius," he said, pointing his ginormous index finger at the top of my head, "doesn't believe this is CCR on the jukebox."

The eight random people in the bar all shook their heads and said, "What?" and "Of course it's CCR."

Tyler continued, "I'm going to Google it and if it's CCR, then this guy will buy this bar a round."

The other daytime drinkers-slash-alcoholics all cheered and clapped. I watched as Tyler Googled it. His silly, smug grin was washed from his face in seconds.

He stared at the screen and then under his breath he said, "It's the goddamn Hollies." He looked around the bar and yelled, "We lost, people. Sorry. Better luck next time."

When things settled down, I remembered that I wanted to interrogate him about the pregnancy-test thing. "Do you and Jenny have any news or anything?"

He looked over at me. "No. Why?"

"I was wondering about the baby thing."

"The baby thing?" He seemed pissed. "Is that how you ask if Jenny's pregnant?"

"Shit. Sorry, bro. I didn't mean to be rude. Yeah, I guess I'm asking if Jenny's pregnant."

"No, she's not, but we're still trying, and I don't mind that part." He waggled his brows. "What about you guys? You gonna wait until after you're married?"

"I don't know. At first we were like rearing to go, but our jets have cooled. We're definitely waiting until after we're married and then some. Dude, it's hard enough having a puppy, and with the studio launching, we'd be crazy to go there. I want kids for sure, but we've got plenty of time."

"Yeah, man. I hear ya. So you guys are getting married in two weeks. That means we have to do the bachelor party next weekend. I've been brainstorming."

"I don't need a bachelor party."

"Hell, yeah, you do, and I have the perfect idea."

"What?"

"Pub crawl and then lap dances." He arched his eyebrows and nodded, saying, "Hmm, hmm, whaddya think?"

"I don't even know what to think. Whatever your plan is, you best run it by Mia. I don't want to be divorced before I'm married."

"All right, then it's set for next Saturday. It will all be planned and I'll tell Mia almost everything."

"No nudey bars or strippers," I said nonchalantly.

"That's like a rite of passage. What's happened to you?" Tyler's long arms started waving around. He normally talked with his hands, but when he was really passionate about something he would get both arms into it. It was creepy.

"I just don't want to."

"Liar."

Standing up from my stool, I threw a five-dollar bill down on the bar. "There. I'll get mine. Everyone thinks that song is by Creedence Clearwater Revival; don't sweat it. I gotta bolt."

I gave Tyler a typical guy shoulder hug and headed out the door. I heard him call back, "I'll see you at eight on Saturday!"

Before heading up to our loft, I stopped at the studio. Frank was sitting on the lobby couch, talking boisterously on his cell phone. The lobby was a tiny room in the front of the building. There were no windows aside from the two glass double doors. Inside the lobby sat a small couch and two leather captain's chairs facing an Indian-inspired wooden table that Sheil had given us. There was a small desk in the corner where the receptionist, Maggie, sat. She was always insanely preoccupied with her looks. When I walked in, Frank held a finger up to me. I glanced over at Maggie, who was looking at herself in a compact mirror.

"Mags," I said in a loud whisper. When she looked up, I jetted my thumb toward Frank and mouthed, "Why is he here?"

She shrugged and then went back to applying a coat of lipgloss. *She's grossly overpaid.*

I took a seat next to Frank and waited for him to wrap up the call.

"Saturday, yes, that should work," he said into the phone before pressing End and slipping it into his pocket.

He took his fedora off and placed it on the table. This was a sign that Frank had something important to tell me. He leaned forward and clasped his hands between his knees.

"You really cannot control yourself, can you?" he said calmly.

"What are you talking about?"

"That was Chad's lawyer. She's a mean bitch, Will."

I took a deep breath and shook my head. "He doesn't have a case."

"Apparently they're trying to bring assault charges against you. Chad's inner ear is damaged from your little tantrum. Singers usually need their hearing intact, Will."

My heart started racing. "There is no fucking way in hell that I fucked up that kid's ear."

"They have an eye witness that said you dragged him around the studio by his ear."

"Oh my God, this is insane. I barely tugged on it. He's lying. The kid wanted credit for our songs, and he couldn't even play 'Mary Had a Little Lamb.' Frank, this is bullshit."

"Live Wire contacted me, wanted some insight, and then gave the lawyer my number, but this is totally out of my league. You better lawyer up. You have a meeting this Saturday, and I think you'll probably want representation."

I was stunned. "My bachelor party is Saturday," I said quietly to myself.

"His lawyer is from Topeka, the town where the kid is from. I guess it's his great aunt or something. She can only be here Saturday. You better work it out. They'll be here at ten a.m. to take a statement." He said the last part as he stood, placing his fedora back on his head.

I was completely quiet and still as a statue as Frank

left the building. I glanced back at Maggie.

"You're screwed," she said.

"Thank you, master of the obvious."

Her face scrunched up with pity. "Sorry."

"It's five o'clock, Mags, you can go."

I went around shutting off lights and locking doors. Walking through the sound room, I paused at the piano and thought about Mia writing that song for Chad. Even though Mia rarely wrote lyrics, I would always ask her what the music was about, what she was thinking of when she wrote a piece. She said the song for Chad, which we'd eventually titled Lost N Found, was about the people we encounter in life who just tarry along, never really letting anyone get to know them. It's those people who don't understand what loyalty means; they bounce from one set of friends to another, never building strong bonds. They're like the pieces of paper floating around at the wind's mercy.

I sat at the bench and began playing it. We had written lyrics and then tweaked them to fit Chad's vocals and image, but the original was ten times more meaningful. I felt the conflict rise in me again. This is what I wanted, the normalcy of coming to the same place every day, of having a stable job, but whenever we had to give away a piece of ourselves through the songs, I felt like a sellout. I sang the original quietly to myself that night as I played Mia's beautiful music.

Gravity has got the best of me.
She takes a hold,
won't let me go.
She rips me into pieces.

Coming home,
I'm left alone with nothing but a box
of mismatched socks
and missing puzzle pieces.

I'm lost but never found.
I'm riding the wind
and coming down
until I'm swept away again.

You've said cut ties.
You've said count lies.
Break your best intentions and leave no trace.
All the hurt can be erased if you stay with me on the
surface.

I'm lost but never found.
I'm riding the wind
and coming down
until I'm swept away again.

That song had way too much depth and meaning for a fuckwit like Chad. I wasn't at all bummed he wouldn't get to sing it. I had no idea what would happen with the lawsuit, but I chose that night to keep it to myself and wait until after the wedding to bring it up with Mia.

I shuffled up the stairs to our loft with the weight of the world on my shoulders. As soon as I opened the door, a sweet scent flooded my senses. It smelled like Mia had been baking. The only light on in the apartment was coming from above the stove. It was seven o'clock, but it appeared Mia had already gone to bed. I walked into the kitchen area with June bouncing around at my feet. I picked her up and leaned over the stove. Wrapped in cellophane were three chocolate croissants. Mia had been baking goodies like that most of her life during the summers when she would come to New York and work in her father's café. She rarely ever made stuff like that at home. I slid one out and devoured it while June tried ineffectively to chomp off a piece. She squirmed around in my arms.

"Why aren't you in your crate?" I said to her. She looked at me with her big, round puppy-dog eyes. "I'm a sucker, I would have let you out too."

I headed down the short hallway. We called our apartment a loft because it had one large room with high, gabled ceilings. The walls that separated the bedrooms and bathroom didn't reach the ceiling, so essentially we lived in a loft with some walls.

Our bedroom was dark but there was enough light coming from the hallway that I could see Mia curled up under the covers. I went to her side. Once I moved out of the doorway, the light shone on her face. She was sound asleep at seven o'clock. I took a quick shower and slid into bed in my boxers. She stirred and opened her eyes just a crack.

"Hi, baby," she said. "What time is it?"

"It's seven fifteen."

"Oh my gosh. I was just gonna take a little nap. I made croissants," she mumbled, then yawned with her eyes still closed.

"I had one. They're delicious."

She scooted toward me, sank down and then nestled into my chest. We wrapped our arms around each other. She was so warm, like a little oven.

"Do you want me to get up and make dinner?"

"No, I had a long day. I just want to lie here with you," I said.

"I've been exhausted too."

"Is Jenny making you crazy with the wedding planning?"

"Kind of." She said it in a way that made me think she didn't want to put Jenny down. Mia was insanely loyal; she never talked shit about people even though we both knew Jenny was driving her mad.

"She's not pregnant," I said.

"I know. It sucks."

"It will happen for them." A few seconds later, I laughed to myself, thinking about Tyler in the bar earlier that day.

"What are you laughing about?"

"Today Tyler and I got into a debate over who sings a song. He got everyone in the bar involved."

She rolled over and tucked herself into me so that I was spooning her. "What song?"

"Long Cool Woman in a Black Dress."

Through a yawn she said, "Oh that's the Hollies."

I laughed quietly and then moments later, I felt her go

boneless. She was asleep. I nuzzled my face into her hair, inhaling her sweet, clean scent. "God, I love you," I whispered.

Saturday morning, with Mia cuddled in my arms, I finally asked her, "What was it that made you come around? When did you know you loved me?"

"I knew the day I met you." She kissed my chest and then laid her head flat again before she started rambling. "I was stupid, Will. It took me a long time to see that. I wish we could take that year back. My father would still be alive and I would just meet you on a flight somewhere. We would meet and decide right then and there to live the rest of our lives together in some paradise, playing music on a beach. You know?"

"I think everything happens for a reason. All those months getting to know you... Even if we weren't together, it meant a lot to me. I don't want to take it back and I don't think you should want to either. I just meant when did it click in your head?"

"When I saw Lauren."

"Who's Lauren?"

"This woman I met in the airport, the same day I met you actually."

Something rang a bell about what Mia was saying, even though we'd never talked about it. "Wait a minute. I met a Lauren in the airport that day too."

"You're kidding?" She sat up in bed and turned toward

me. "A dark-haired woman, kind of a mess? With two little boys?"

"Yes, that's her."

"Crazy coincidence."

"Totally. She was probably on our flight but we didn't notice because we were busy." I smirked.

She laughed. "You make that sound naughty."

"Well?"

"Well, anyway, after L.A., after you said I ruined you... I ran into her at Tompkins Square Park."

The mere mention of Mia breaking my heart in L.A. sent a jolt of terror through my body. "And?"

"And she told me about falling in love with her husband. She said something like you can't know the future for sure; love is having faith in the other person and yourself. It's trusting yourself to know who is right for you. Something did click after that. I tried to get a hold of you."

"I know. I'm sorry. I just needed to be sure that you weren't..." I swallowed.

"What, Wilbur? That I wasn't what?" she said with a playful smirk.

I began tickling her, pinching at her sides and behind her knees until she was flat on her back, writhing around. I hovered over her and held her arms braced above her head.

"I needed to make sure you weren't fucking with my heart again, you little tease." I ducked my head and ran my tongue up her neck and continued the torture up her cheek and to her forehead.

She squirmed, screaming, "Yuck! Let me go!"

We were laughing hysterically until finally we were

cuddled up again, dozing off with the morning light blasting us through the window.

TRACK 4: Bros before Hos

M ia was gone when I woke up again. She'd left me a note saying she was going to a dress fitting with Jenny. I looked at the clock. It was nine forty-five. I got dressed and bolted down to the studio where Frank was already waiting outside.

"I think you should have hired a lawyer, Will."

"Look, I'm not talking today. We'll let them say their piece. I've seen nothing yet to make me think I need to hire a lawyer. No charges, no court papers. This is a scare tactic."

"I hope you're right." As I unlocked the door, I noticed someone walking toward us in the reflection.

"Charlene Fretas," Frank said loudly. "I'm Frank Abedo." He was reaching out to shake her hand as I turned to introduce myself. I immediately froze, as did she.

I had met Charlene months before Mia and I had gotten together. She'd come into the bar I used to work in and basically propositioned me. I'd initially turned her down, but then after a long, depressing night of putting up with obnoxious bimbos at a club and feeling utter rejection from Mia, I'd given in and met Charlene—Charlie—in her hotel room.

She was quite a bit older and she had told me that she was a lawyer in town for business. When I'd gone to her room that night, I'd fully expected to find a sex- crazed cougar. In fact, I was kind of hoping for it after learning about Mia and her then-boyfriend. Instead, Charlie and I had done nothing but basically spill our guts about recent heartbreaks. Past the rock-hard exterior, she was kind and compassionate. We'd cuddled. It sounds stupid, but we just slept in the same bed and held each other. It was exactly what I'd needed at the time.

She was not the person I expected to see that day outside my studio. I could tell right away that she was wearing her lawyer hat because she barely broke a smile when she saw my face. "Mr. Ryan," she said to me as she shook my hand.

"Charlie," I replied.

"It's Charlene. Let's keep this professional."

The memory of our night together vanished. Showing up at my studio and threatening to sue on behalf of Chad annihilated any respect I'd had for her.

"Okay, fine. Charlene it is. So, Charlene, you're Chad's lawyer?"

"Yes, and I'm also his aunt. I wanted to get that on the record."

"Duly noted. Although, I heard you're his *great* aunt?" I said, smirking.

"Yes, great aunt. My sister had his mother when she was fifteen, so that made me a very young aunt."

"That's neither here nor there," Frank said, gesturing toward the door. "Shall we?"

We took seats in the meeting room, which had nothing but a coffee maker and a large oval conference table and chairs. Charlene immediately pulled out a digital recorder.

"No," I said.

She shrugged and then took the battery out and set it next to the recorder on the table. It was a gesture to earn trust.

"I don't even know what this is about, Charlene. Why don't we start with a conversation? Why are you here?"

She leaned back in the chair, scanning me, looking for something, a tell or an angle, I wasn't sure. I raised my eyebrows very slightly, just enough to look playful. She quickly sat upright and focused on the documents in front of her. "We're here because Chad has a promising career in front of him."

"That remains to be seen," I countered quickly.

She pulled a paper from her binder. "He has an inner-ear infection and this is the doctor's note."

I took the note from across the table. There was a list of about twenty possible causes, including the most common at the top: bacteria or virus. Somewhere down the list, I found the word trauma. Someone had highlighted it as if to imply that was the cause.

Trying to remain as cool and collected as possible, I set the paper down and looked up, right into Charlene's eyes. "I had nothing to do with Chad's ear infection, and you know it. Why don't we stop right here, because I know you don't want to blackmail me. That's not your style. Put your cards on the table, and tell me why you're here."

At first it seemed like my words had angered her. She began tapping a paper clip on the table fervently. After a few deep breaths through her nose and out her mouth, she asked calmly, "Will you help my nephew?"

In the same calm voice, I replied, "Not. In. This. Fucking. Lifetime. Or the next."

"Will," Frank said in a no-nonsense tone.

Charlene shook her head for emphasis as she tried to persuade me. "Listen to me, Will, he promised—no more shenanigans. He needs you guys. He's a good kid, he really is, and he looks up to you so much."

"He doesn't need me, he has a record deal. Live Wire will find another producer and studio. It's not a big deal."

"He really wants you guys. He knows what a talent you and your girlfriend are."

"Fiancée."

"Fiancée, of course. Just sit with it for a while. You can decide in a few days."

Frank nodded his head at me as if to say take her up on the offer.

I thought about Mia and how she seemed so concerned with stability. I wondered why I was fighting this kid. I wondered why it sometimes felt like a fight to give up our songs. The one thing I knew in that moment was that no matter what, we had control. I leaned back and crossed my arms. "I will not move forward until I have everything in writing. He has no creative input at all, and I want a higher percentage in royalties."

There were several moments of silence.

Charlie stared at me, chewing on the side of her lip nervously. "You drive a hard bargain, Mr. Ryan, but I think

Chad and the label will agree to your terms," she said with a perfunctory smile.

As I walked her out through the lobby, she stopped when a black-and-white picture on the wall caught her eye. It was Mia sitting on my lap at the piano, both our faces frozen in laughter.

"She's beautiful. What's her name?"

"Mia."

Charlene nodded. "Ah, well, good for you." She stuck her hand out for me to shake. I knew she'd realized it was the girl I was pouring my guts out to her about that night back in the hotel room. "We'll be in touch, Will."

"Bye, Charlie."

She smiled genuinely for the first time and then walked out the door.

My phone buzzed loudly in my pocket. I took a long breath and looked down at the screen. It was Mia and I was relieved the drama was over for the day.

"Hi, babe. How was the fitting?"

"Good. The dress should be perfect."

"I can't wait to see it."

"I want it to be a total surprise."

"Yeah," I said, but I was still preoccupied, thinking about the cluster-fuck that had just transpired over Chad. I should have been happy; it had basically gone in my favor.

"What's wrong, Will?"

"Nothing."

"I thought about you all day today. I just couldn't stop thinking that something was bugging you."

Mia could always sense things. Call it female intuition, who knows, but I couldn't get anything past her. "Why?"

"I don't know, just had a weird feeling."

"I'm okay. Everything's fine and it's all good now. Don't worry."

"You're gonna have fun with the guys tonight, right? By the way, I'm meeting Martha for an early dinner, so I probably won't see you."

"Okay, tell her I said hi. I won't be too late."

"Just have fun, baby," she said vehemently.

"Love you."

"Love you too."

When Tyler got to my apartment, he looked disappointed. Scowling and shaking his head, he said, "What are you wearing?"

I had on a red T-shirt that said "Sup" on it and black jeans. "I like this shirt. What's wrong with it?"

"Don't you have any shirts that don't have writing on them?"

I walked back to my room, tore my shirt off and threw it on the bed. I stared up into my closet.

Tyler came to my room and stood in the doorway. "How do you have fucking abs? You don't even work out."

"You admiring my physique?" I said to him without taking my eyes off the closet.

"It's just not right."

I pulled a plain black T-shirt off the hanger and slipped it over my head. "How's this?"

"Better."

As we headed down the stairs, Tyler yelled back, "We're meeting Josh and Kyle."

"Are you kidding me? I can't stand Josh."

He turned to me just before walking out into the street. "He's fun."

"He acts like a fool. He'll either get into a fight, get kicked out of the bar, or get arrested."

"He hasn't been arrested in two years and anyway, so what if he does? It's entertainment."

He had a point. "Yeah, I guess. Where are we headed?"

"We're meeting the guys at the Red Bar."

"I love that place—they have the best jukebox."

We entered the tiny red bar and found Josh and Kyle sitting at the end. As soon as they spotted us, Josh stood up, threw his pudgy arms into the air and yelled, "Dicks before chicks, man!"

I ducked behind Tyler, shaking my head. In the five seconds it took us to reach Josh and Kyle at the end of the bar, they had already ordered me an Irish Car Bomb. After high fives and fist bumps, Josh pushed the beer and shot toward me and started chanting, "Chug, chug, chug."

Josh was a cross between Chris Farley and Jack Nicholson. He was overweight with plenty of stupid energy, but he had these really exaggerated eyebrows and an overbearing forehead, which gave a permanently sinister look to his face.

I dropped the shot in the beer and downed the whole thing in three huge gulps, then slammed it back down on the bar.

Kyle, who was always with Josh, was the perfectly innocent sidekick. He was skinny, blond, and a virgin at the age of thirty, which basically made him the butt of all jokes. He and Josh were Tyler's old roommates. They'd met in college when all three of them worked part time at Subway. They still called themselves sandwich artists—ridiculous.

Kyle was a decent-enough-looking guy, so it was hard to understand how he hadn't gotten with at least one girl. The only explanation I could come up with was that he was always with Josh, who was the female deflector. In bars, women wouldn't come within ten feet of Josh, yet he always found a way to get a girlfriend. At the time, he was dating a belly dancer he'd met while she was performing at a Mediterranean restaurant.

"Speaking of chicks, how's your girl, Josh?"

"She's great. She's working tonight. You guys want to go check her out?"

"Uh, no," Tyler said.

Josh objectified his own girlfriend in the strangest way and then told everyone she liked it, another reason I couldn't stand him.

"What's her name again, bro?" I asked.

This time Kyle chimed in. "Saphir!" he blurted out.

Josh turned toward him and glared before turning back to Tyler and me. "That's her stage name. And Kyle here got to see her perform last weekend."

"Did I ever," Kyle said dreamily.

Josh elbowed him.

"Is that an Indian name?" I asked.

"Her real name is Brittney. She's from Kentucky, total white girl, but man, she can shake it. You know what I mean?" He wiggled his Jack Nicholson eyebrows.

"Nice," I said, smiling sarcastically.

"Kyle, when are you gonna go for it?"

"Go for what?" The question terrified him.

"What do you think?" Tyler said.

"I'm waiting for the right girl," he replied in a squeaky voice before taking a large gulp of beer. He was tapping his fingers on the bar nervously.

"She's cute." I pointed to a small, unintimidating-looking woman standing a few feet away, trying to get the bartender's attention. "Why don't you go buy her a drink?"

"You should," Josh blurted out. "I'll help you."

"No!" Tyler and I yelled in unison.

Josh didn't listen and Kyle just sat there, eyes opened as wide as they could go. Josh stood up on his toes to see over the other patrons blocking his view of the tiny, short-haired blonde. "Hey, hottie!" he yelled.

"Oh, God." I planted my face in my palms over the bar.

"Yeah, you, Tinker Bell. My buddy here wants to buy your sweet ass a drink."

"Christ," Tyler mumbled.

Kyle literally sank within himself on the stool. His expression was nothing short of horrified. The girl shook her head and moved farther down the bar, away from us.

"Way to go, dickwad." I said to Josh.

"What? That chick was a bitch. I saved Kyle from some serious heartache." He smacked Kyle on the back.

"Ouch. I don't need your help, Josh. You fucking cock block me every time we're out. What is your problem?"

"Time for more shots!" Josh announced.

Several hours of irresponsible binge drinking went on before the shit hit the fan. Apparently while Tyler and I sat unaware, arguing over where to get the best pizza, Kyle and Josh were having a heart-to-heart. It started when Josh apologized for the scene earlier with Tinker Bell. The conversation went on and on, both of them professing their drunken love for each other while Tyler and I continued an old argument about the difference between yams and sweet potatoes—that's the kind of profound shit Tyler and I talked about. We were startled back to reality when we heard Josh shout, "What the fuck?"

"*She* came on to *me*," Kyle said with his hands up defensively.

Josh went toward him in what appeared to be the universal gesture for *I am going to kill you by strangulation* while yelling, "You didn't have to fuck her."

"Oh, shit, you fucked the belly dancer?" Tyler said to Kyle.

At the same time, Josh blurted out "Brittney" while Kyle yelled "Saphir."

The men immediately started rolling around on the ground, trying to kill each other while Tyler tried to break it up. As hard as it was, I managed to ignore all the commotion.

I yelled to the bartender, who was looking on in disbelief. I shrugged. "It's my bachelor party."

He nodded. "Right on. Congrats, man. Are those your friends?"

"No!" I yelled back. I paid for all the drinks, another downside to hanging out with idiots, and then I walked outside and gave a homeless guy four dollars for one cigarette.

Tyler followed shortly after. "That was crazy."

"Are they still fighting in there?" I said, blowing a lungful of smoke into the air.

"No, Kyle escaped out the back door while Josh was puking behind the bar. He'll be kicked out for sure. It's only a matter of seconds."

Sure enough, ten seconds later, two burly bouncers came out, dragging Josh between them.

"We'll take it from here, boys," I said before turning and flagging down a cab. "I'll walk home. Do you want to get Josh to his place?"

"Will, this is your bachelor party—we've only been to one bar. We have a couple more stops on the agenda."

"Dude, I'm done. I'm over it."

Josh stood between us, swaying. "That bitch cheated on me," he slurred. "Stupid whore. Im'a kill her... and him."

"Whoa, Josh, settle down," Tyler said. "We're gonna get you home." Tyler turned his attention toward me. "Will, you have to come with me. What if he passes out?"

"You're fucking huge; you'll manage."

"I can't lift three hundred pounds of dead weight."

"Take me to find Brittney. Please, guys."

"No, we're taking you home." I barked, "You can cry all you want, but no one is going to die over a skanky belly dancer."

"Why you callin' her a skank, man?" he said and then began weeping like a baby.

We managed to shove Josh into the back of a cab. Tyler got in after him, and I slipped into the front seat. Josh mumbled his address and then farted and burped at the same time. I spent the rest of the drive to Josh's house with my head out the window.

Unbelievably, when we reached his apartment, he was able to fully navigate his rotund body up the narrow staircase to his door. After we made sure he was safely inside, we went out to the cab and got in the back.

"Seriously, Tyler, I think I'm done."

"I have a surprise for you." He whispered something to the cabbie. The man nodded.

"I'm tired."

"All you have to do is sit there and watch."

"No. I said no strippers."

"Be quiet, pussy."

When we pulled up in front of my loft and studio building, I turned to Tyler. "You're dropping me off at home. Is that the big surprise?"

We hopped out; Tyler told the cabbie to wait. He pulled a set of keys from his pocket and began unlocking the door to the studio. The first thing I noticed was that the alarm didn't go off.

"What are we doing? Please tell me you didn't hire strippers to come here."

"What are friends for? Come on, it would be a waste of money if you didn't go back there and at least sneak a peek." He patted me on the back and then pulled a flask from his jacket pocket. "Here, you might need this. It's whiskey—only the finest."

"Tyler, I don't know about this."

"Just go back there. Take a seat in the control room." When I took the flask from his hands and entered the lobby, he said, "Have fun."

"Wait a minute, you're not going in there with me?"

"No way, this is all for you," he said before abruptly shutting the door and locking me in. He strolled back to the cab, and then without looking back, he threw his hand up and waved good-bye.

TRACK 5: Breathe

I shook my head, took a larger-than-necessary swig from the flask, and began heading down the long hallway to the control room. It was so dark that I had to feel my way over to the light switch. I brushed the switch plate with my hand and noticed that someone had placed tape over it, preventing me from turning the light on.

Then I heard a female voice whisper, "Uh uh," over the control-room speakers. I felt my way to the sound board and chair and sat down. I was squinting, trying to see inside the sound room, when the music began playing. Even though there were no lights blinking on the board, I still felt around for the buttons and knobs but quickly realized the equipment in the control room was off except for one microphone feed.

Whoever was in the sound room had control of the music. I recognized the song right away from the humming in the beginning. It was "Retrograde" by James Blake. The sound room remained dark until the first clapping beat of the song. What happened next is hard for me to put into words, but goddammit, I'll try.

Right at that first beat, a small light went on overhead on the other side of the glass. The dim spotlight shone down into an empty space in the middle of the sound room until a woman very slowly and seductively stepped into the light. She was wearing a short, black lace dress, so short I could see the black garters peeking out from underneath. Feeling my heart rate increase, I wiped my sweating palms on my jeans and rocked back in my chair nervously.

She threw her leg up onto the piano bench and then ran both hands up her thigh, raising the dress even higher. With ease, she reached down and removed her black stiletto heel, setting it on the bench beside her foot. She raised her dress again and unbuckled the garter from the leg still perched on the bench. In painfully slow motion, she rolled the material down and off her foot before tossing it into the darkness. I could see bright red nail polish on her fingers and toes, the same shade of red she wore on her lips. It was like the overhead light created this illusion that the woman was in one of those black and white photos where only a few objects are colored in. Her skin was radiant and glowing against her dark, almost black hair. She put her heel back on and then repeated the same torturous motion on the other leg as I watched in complete awe.

Her beauty took my breath away and the way she moved and the music—I was about to come undone. I took another swig of whiskey. She approached the glass, slowly unzipping the side of her dress as she moved. Her eyes were fixed on mine. Her pouty lips were just barely open. Standing two feet from the glass, she slid the shoulder of her dress off one side and the whole thing fell to the ground. Her dark hair, curled in loose ringlets, fell back on her shoulders, caressing the tops of her breasts. She turned around and, with her back to me, unclasped her bra, tossing it aside. She gripped her garter belt and thong on each hip and bent over to slide them down her legs. Her perfect ass was right at my eye level.

She strutted away from the glass, never turning around until she reached the piano bench. Her movements were so graceful and seductive, like she had been stripping for years. She turned to face me as she straddled the bench. I watched her expression change from alluring and provocative to playful. A sweet, knowing smile flashed across her face. With her legs spread, totally exposed, she pointed her finger at the glass and summoned me. It was my beautiful, lovely Mia, sitting there wearing nothing but her heels, waiting for me to take her.

I could barely walk I was so turned on. Still disoriented, I fumbled my way through the door into the sound room and past several instruments and chairs until I was standing over her at the piano. Her position, perched naked on the bench, looking up at me through her big, beautiful hazel eyes, was so vulnerable and sweet. Yet I knew Mia was very much in control.

"That was the fucking hottest thing I've ever seen, baby."

She laughed, a blush creeping over her cheeks. "I can tell," she said, her gaze moving to the belt on my jeans.

"You have to play that song again so I can act out everything I was imagining behind the glass."

She stood up, her feet still on each side of the bench.

"It's on repeat," she whispered as she undid the buckle of my belt.

With her legs spread, I could feel the heat radiating from her body. It was as though my hand had a mind of its own. I reached down and touched her, gently at first and in just the right spot. She sucked in a quick breath and then closed her eyes and moaned quietly. I placed my other hand on her hip and then slid it up her smooth sides, touching her breast, circling her nipple and then up farther until I was holding her neck and kissing her mouth. My other hand stayed at work on Mia as she made approving sounds against my lips. I could feel her pressing herself against me, harder, wanting more.

"I'm ready," she said in a breathy voice.

I wondered in that moment if it would be shallow of me to like that part of Mia the best, the part of her that liked to plan secret stripteases and let me touch her all over. I'm a guy, after all. When we were together, kissing and touching, it was like playing music. She always knew what move to make, like she was subconsciously counting beats from a sheet of music. We were always so in sync that it felt like we'd been together for centuries, but in a good way. I was convinced we had lived twenty thousand lives, and in each one, we had found each other, like two tiny magnets in a drawer the size of the universe. She and I fit and moved together with such ease, I couldn't imagine ever being with anyone else.

By the time I pulled away from her mouth, we were both naked. When I picked her up, she straddled me. Her perfect little legs were tightened around my waist like a vise, leaving little work for my arms. I moved to the wall and pressed her against the soundproofing material. Who knew those puffy little foam spikes could make wall screwing ten times better? I moved inside her as she settled on me until we were flush. I didn't hesitate to press her hard against the wall. Our bodies melded together so effortlessly, moving with the rhythm of our mouths kissing and sucking.

She broke away from the kiss and pressed her head against the wall. Looking up and arching her back, she closed her eyes and called out a song of sounds: whimpers and moans, loud breaths and blissful cries so sweet and uninhibited that I couldn't stop the waves crashing over me as I slammed into her. Against the wall, shivering like it was our first time, we both cried out.

I knelt down, still holding her against me, still inside her. She rested her head on my shoulder as we sat there embracing each other for several moments, trying to catch our breaths.

"Will?" she said in her melodic voice.

"Yes, baby."

"I'm pregnant."

Well if those two words didn't throw this boy for a loop...

I leaned back so that I could look her in the eye.

"I don't think it works that way, kitten. It usually takes a few weeks before one even has symptoms." *First stage: denial.*

She took a deep breath through her nose and smiled piteously at me. "I don't mean I got pregnant just now. I was already pregnant. I found out last week."

"And you let me do that to you? What I just did... to

you... against the wall?" I pointed frantically behind her. *Second stage: anger.*

"It's okay to have sex when you're pregnant." She cupped my face. She was smiling, and then I saw a hint of sadness wash over her.

"I thought you were getting on the pill. I thought you were on the pill. Aren't you on the pill?" *Stage three: bargaining.* In those moments after she told me, I had no clear stream of consciousness. I was simply spewing out every word that popped into my head.

"I never got a chance to start the pills." Her eyes filled with tears.

"Are we going to be able to handle a baby and the expenses and... oh my God... everything will have to change because of *this*." I gestured with my hand toward her stomach as I held her out, away from my body. *Stage four: depression.*

Tears were now streaming steadily down her face. Her eyes were scrunched up with such an expression of pain dragging them down that it made my heart ache. She sniffled and wiped her cheeks with the back of her hand. "I'm sorry, Will. I thought you wanted *this* with me." She looked down at her stomach the same way I had. "I'm sorry." She put her face in her hands and began to sob. I was officially the biggest asshole in the world. She was curled up in my arms, naked, sobbing, heartbroken, and pregnant with my child.

I watched her cry for several moments. She let me pull her closer so I could soothe her even though I was the cause of her pain. There was something so beautiful about her raw vulnerability, but it hurt to know I had caused her to feel that way.

"I love you," I said.

"I'm sorry," she replied.

At first the news of her pregnancy seemed life changing in a scary way, but those thoughts were fleeting. Sitting there with her crying in my arms, I realized our baby, which we had made together, was growing inside her. Once it became tangible in my mind, her being pregnant became the most life-affirming news I had ever received.

"No, I'm sorry." I started kissing her all over. "I love this baby. This is our baby," I said as I kissed her belly and breasts and neck. "I'm so happy, Mia. I realize this is all I've ever wanted, to be with you and to make a family." *Stage five: acceptance.*

I'm not sure why I had to weather the stages of grief after hearing the news that night. Maybe it was the death of my singledom or the death of my own childhood that scared me. For some reason, when you're faced with the realization that you're going to become a parent, it immediately changes how you view yourself. You no longer think of yourself as someone else's child because you can't be a parent and a child. It's an official good-bye, and good-byes always scared the hell out of me.

I continued kissing her as she cried and cried and cried, until finally there were no more tears.

She looked up at me with puffy red eyes and said, "Really?"

"Really what?"

"You really want this?"

"Yes." I brushed the hair out of her face. "I promise. It

just took me a second to process it. I'm sorry I reacted that way. You know I want this with you, Mia."

She nodded unconvincingly and then stood up and reached for her dress.

"No, here," I said and handed her my black T-shirt. "We'll clean this up tomorrow. Let's get you to bed."

We exchanged few words as we scurried, half naked, out of the studio and into the freezing air. The doorway into the loft stairwell was only a few feet away.

"I'm freezing. I want to take a bath," she said as we ran up the steps.

Inside the loft, I immediately went in and drew a bath for her. "Are you allowed to takes baths?" I yelled from the bathroom as she tinkered around in the kitchen.

"Yes, it just can't be too hot," she said finally as she approached me from the hallway. She had a stack of books in her hand.

"What are those?"

"Some pregnancy and childbirth books Martha gave me."

I immediately shut the water off and stood up from the side of the tub. "What?" I barked. There were so many things running through my mind in that moment.

"Calm down, Will."

"You told Martha before you told me?" I was shocked.

She held her ground. "Hold on a minute—just listen. I went to the café to visit Martha that day you came by, remember?"

I nodded.

"I was complaining to her about... you know, girl stuff?"

"No, I don't know. Martha is not a girl, she's sixty-six. What were you telling her?"

"I told her my nipples were sore, okay?" She blushed all the way to her toes and then stalked off to our bedroom.

"Wait, Mia, hold on. Aren't you gonna take a bath?"

"Yes, but I don't want you berating me in there."

I huffed. "Just tell me the story."

She sat on the edge of our bed with a pouty face and then she got all misty-eyed again.

"Don't cry."

"I'm not!" She punched the sides of the bed. "I'm just embarrassed."

"Baby, you're gonna have to get over that very soon. You can tell me when your nipples hurt, for Christ's sake."

"Will," she whined. "It's not that, but even if I did tell you, you wouldn't know what it meant."

"That brings me to my next question. How does Martha know about any of this stuff? She doesn't even have kids."

"Martha's a doula. I thought you knew that."

"She's a whata?"

Mia shook her head and exhaled, looking down at her hands in her lap. She brought her thumb up to her mouth.

"Oh, no. You are not chewing on that thumb." I pulled her hand away.

"A doula is like a birth assistant. She's there for pregnant women before, during and after childbirth."

"So, what, like a nurse?"

"Doulas mostly assist natural or home births. I want to have this baby naturally, no drugs."

"Are you kidding me? You love drugs."

RENÉE CARLINO

"God, Will, be serious for once."

I slapped my hand to my bare chest. "I am. I'm as serious as a fucking heart attack, Mia. Why would you want to put yourself through that torture?"

"I just want to see if I can do it. I want to see what I'm made of."

"It's masochistic. One of my sisters had a baby naturally and she said she would never do it again. She said it was like being blown apart from inside out."

"Thanks a lot for that visual." She crossed her arms.

"Sorry, but it's true. You need to know."

"Listen, Martha has been present for hundreds of births and she says natural is way safer for the baby and me."

"It's safer?" That got my attention.

She held a book out to me titled *The Birth That's Right for You*. "Yeah, it basically says that in here."

"Well then, if it's safer, by all means." I took the book from her hands and flipped through it. "Oh, you're not even gonna get a Tylenol, lady. It says every intervention you add increases your chance of having a C-section." I waved my index finger at her. "No drugs for you."

She laughed.

"And... and you are going to breast-feed that kid for at least five years. You know how much bad crap is in cow's milk?" I was being silly at that point, but it looked like Mia was relieved and that's all that mattered.

She smiled. "Let's not go too far, buddy."

"You still haven't told me what happened, how Martha found out." I sat down next to her on the bed.

She took my hand in hers. "That day at the café when I

60

told Martha about my... you know..."

"Yes, your nipples, Mia. Let's stop being embarrassed. I get sore nipples all the time."

"Really?"

"No," I said seriously.

She elbowed me. "She said I should go buy a pregnancy test and go up to Jenny's and take it. I didn't think Jenny was home. It was actually kind of awful. Right after I texted you, I used my key to get into her apartment where I found her crying on the couch. She said she saw me in the store, buying the test. She ran home and that's where I found her."

"Oh my God, poor Jenny."

"Remember when Jenny had the miscarriage and you said that it would change her?" I nodded and Mia continued, "Well, now she has a really hard time hearing about other people getting pregnant. She doesn't even like to see pregnant women on the street. She insisted on me taking the test—it was like she wanted to punish herself. We got into a huge fight because I didn't want take it in front of her. She went completely aggro. There were two tests in the box, so I peed on both and handed her one as I left the apartment. On the way down the stairwell, I looked at the test and saw that it was positive."

"Why didn't you tell me? And how did Martha know?"

"I didn't tell you because it seemed like you had a lot on your mind that day. I never told Martha anything definite, but somehow she knew. The next morning, she showed up here with a stack of books and some prenatal vitamins. She has that weird sixth sense, you know?"

"Yeah, she does. What about Jen? How is she?"

"I went to see her after Martha's visit. I sat on her couch and let her cry in my lap for an hour. She promised she wouldn't say anything to Tyler until I told you. Before I left, she told me congratulations. She said she was happy for us and that she hoped we could be pregnant together."

"Aw, man, that must be rough for them."

"Yeah."

We sat there in silence for several moments, absorbing our new reality. "Are you ready for your bath, mama?"

"Will, please do not call me that."

In the tiniest, scariest, robot-baby voice I chanted, "Mama, mama, mama, mama," as I followed Mia into the bathroom.

"Stop, Will."

"Better get used to it, sweet thing."

TRACK 6: Dresses & Dry Toast

A s we approached the big day, Mia became more and more nervous. She had decided we should wait until our wedding to make the pregnancy announcement so she could tell her mom and step-dad in person. Being one of thirteen kids and the youngest after a brother and eleven sisters, baby news was nothing new in my family, but I decided to wait so everyone would hear it at the same time. Except, of course, Tyler, Jenny, and Martha.

Jenny warned Mia to wait until the three-month mark when it was more of a sure thing. Understandably, Jenny was a bit of cynic when it came to these things. Mia said Jenny was practical; I called it negative. Finally, I told Mia she had to make the announcement at the wedding. There was no way anyone would buy any excuse that Mia wasn't drinking at her own wedding other than being pregnant. I argued that everyone would know anyway, so we might as well announce it.

The Thursday before our wedding, I woke up early. It was dawn and the light coming through the window was a dull blue. It was peaceful, like a fading memory. That is until I realized the bed was empty next to me. I flew to my feet, threw on a pair of boxers, and darted out into the hallway.

I heard a small, sickly voice coming from the bathroom behind me. "I'm here." I turned and saw Mia hanging over the toilet. She was pale and her eyes were bloodshot.

"Oh baby, what happened?" I started panicking. "What is it?"

She looked up at me with a painful smile. "I feel like... I feel like, remember that time when you bet Tyler you could drink a fifth of vodka and still play 'Voodoo Child' without missing a note?"

"Yeah, I did, twice, with my eyes closed, and I sang it too. I won a hundred bucks. I felt great."

"No." She paused to dry heave. "Remember how you felt the next morning? Remember, you thought you were dying? You made me write a letter to your family."

"Oh yeah, I felt like shit."

"That's how I feel."

"Really? That bad, huh? I'm not gonna sugarcoat it, baby, you look like death warmed over."

"Thanks."

"You're still beautiful. It's just, there's this green tint to your skin." When she dry heaved again, I asked, "Should I call a doctor? You're gonna be one very unhappy bride on Saturday if you're still feeling this."

"I know. Just call Martha. I'm pretty sure I'm okay. I think I'm experiencing that phenomenon known as morning sickness."

I kissed her on top of the head. "I'll call her right now." I walked into the bedroom, picked up our landline, and dialed Martha.

She didn't even say hello. "Is she having morning sickness?" The sixth sense thing was getting creepy.

"Yeah, she's in the bathroom, throwing up. She doesn't look so good." I went back to the doorway of the bathroom and found Mia hunched on the floor.

"You need to get some food in her."

I held the phone away from my ear and said, "You want me to make you some eggs, baby?"

"No!" Mia and Martha both shouted.

"What should I make her?"

"Just get her some crackers or dry toast. She may need to sleep with crackers and water on the nightstand. She should never let her stomach go empty. Nothing will sound good to her if she lets it get to this point. Make her eat some crackers and drink some club soda if you have it. I'll be over in a bit."

"Thanks, Martha."

"Of course, dear."

Mia was still on the bathroom floor moaning when Martha arrived. She walked in with a satchel full of natural remedies. She had ginger and peppermint tea and some aromatherapy candles and creams. After laying each item on the kitchen bar, she finally addressed me.

"Will, I think it's important that you're involved in every phase of the pregnancy with Mia. Here are some items that should help. I have to get to Kell's."

Mia moaned loudly from down the hall before yelling, "No, Martha, you have to stay."

"Yeah, I think you should stay. I don't know what to do for her."

"That is your baby she's carrying inside her. That is your baby making her sick." She pointed to the items on the counter again and said, "Figure this stuff out."

I stood there stunned as I watched Martha walk hurriedly to the door and leave. I moved with trepidation down the hall. Mia was now lying on a stack of towels, curled up in the fetal position.

"Baby, let me get you into bed."

"Uh uh. I think I'm gonna be sick again."

"I'll bring you a bowl. You can't be comfortable like this." I helped her to her feet and into our room, and then I pulled the covers back for her to slide into bed. "I'll bring you some toast and tea."

When I came back, she was sleeping soundly. Poor girl had probably been up since four a.m. I left the tray of toast and tea on the bedside table and proceeded to light a few candles. After calling the studio and letting them know I would be in late, I plugged my headphones into my iPod and put on the album *Veneer* by José González. I rested the headphones on Mia's belly and proceeded to have the first music lesson and heart-to-heart with my unborn child.

"Listen, kid, you can't be making your mom sick all the time. Here's some soothing music to calm you both." When I kissed her belly, she stirred a bit and then opened her eyes.

"Toast," she mumbled.

"Sit up, Mia."

She sat up, grabbed the piece of toast from my hand,

and shoved it into her mouth ravenously.

"Slow down, you're gonna make yourself sick again."

"I'm starving," she grumbled through a mouthful of bread. She took three tiny sips of ginger tea, closed her eyes, and fell asleep again.

I spent the rest of the morning lying next to her in bed. I read the first several chapters of *What to Expect When You're Expecting* and *The Birth That's Right for You.*

Later that day when she finally woke, her eyes shot open. She looked at me curiously as I stood over her with my arms crossed.

"Have you been taking your folic acid?" I asked.

"Yes," she said, looking confused.

"And you know that when you have a headache, you cannot take ibuprofen?"

"Okay."

"And no hot baths, no sushi, no unpasteurized cheese, and absolutely no alcohol!"

"I heard from someone that pregnant women can have a small glass of wine once in a while."

"Who is this someone? That's hogwash!" I blurted out.

Through disbelief and laughter Mia said, "What?"

"That is simply not true. There is no magic number for what is safe—it's best to avoid alcohol all together."

"What have you been up to, Will?" She eyed me speculatively.

"I've just been reading, that's all."

She got up slowly from the bed, still staring into my eyes. "You have that neurotic look about you right now."

"I think we should start going for thirty-minute walks twice a day."

"Are you worried about me getting fat?"

"God, no." I shook my head. "Natural birth is like a sporting event, Mia. Think of me as your trainer."

"Did you read that whole book?" She pointed to the nightstand.

"I read enough for now. I know exactly what I need to do. In addition to the breast tenderness and nausea, have you been experiencing frequent urination and sensitivity to smells?"

"Um...yes?"

"I need a definitive answer." I was impressed by my ability to not crack a smile.

Mia continued eyeing me. I think she was waiting for me to break into laughter, but I didn't. "Yes. The answer is yes, Dr. Neurotic, why do you ask?"

I tilted my head to the side and squinted, examining her from head to toe. "I believe you are most definitely pregnant. Our next step is to call your OB/GYN and schedule an appointment to confirm it with a blood test and transvaginal ultrasound."

That's when Mia lost it. She plopped back down on the bed, holding her stomach and laughing hysterically.

"Oh my God, Will, you are killing me with this act." She could barely speak. "How do you know all that stuff?"

"This is no act. I'm a quick study. Martha inspired me to get involved, and that's what I'm doing." I smiled finally.

"I don't want you going overboard," she said as she walked to the bathroom to brush her teeth for the tenth time that day.

I always felt like Mia grounded me. If I spent too much time alone with my thoughts, I would let them get the best of me.

"You look like you're feeling better."

She looked into the mirror with a mouthful of toothpaste and nodded. She rinsed her mouth and turned to face me. "What time is it?"

"One o'clock."

Wrapping her arms around my waist, she nuzzled her face into my bare chest. Her sneaky fingers found their way to my belt buckle. She pulled it open and then ran her hand down the front of my jeans and took a hold of me.

I took a step back and eyed her with my arms crossed in front of me. "What are you doing?"

"What does it look like?"

"We can't do it. You're in a delicate state."

"Your body disagrees with you." She smirked and squeezed me tighter. "Plus, you cannot treat me like I'm breakable for nine months. I'll go crazy."

I pulled her hand away. "The answer is no, for now."

"You won't last long," she said, challenging me.

"Watch me," I said, but I knew she was right.

I turned, went into our closet, and grabbed my white T-shirt that said "Diva" on the front of it in black block letters. I pulled it over my head as I spoke to Mia. "I'm going down to the studio for a bit. Everyone has left for the day, so I wanted to work on a few things."

"I'm gonna see if I can get into the doctor this afternoon since our parents will be here tomorrow. Do you want to come to the appointment if I can get in today?"

"Absolutely." I turned and hugged her and then pulled

back and looked her in the eye. "I'm really excited and happy, and I can't wait to marry you and tell everyone about the baby."

"Me too."

I headed down to the empty studio and worked a little bit on Chad's songs at the sound board, and then I went into the sound room with an old Fender Stratocaster that Martha's husband had loaned me. It had this chime-y but rich sound to it when I played the neck. I plugged in, closed my eyes, and began to play the beginning of Led Zeppelin's "Ramble On." I tried to layer in both guitar parts as best I could by adding extra reverb, but the baseline was definitely missing. I kept my eyes closed and tried to imagine the baseline and pattering percussion in the beginning of the song, and then I actually heard it. I opened my eyes and saw Mia standing in the sound room, just feet away from me, tapping the beat on the back of a leather office chair. She was bobbing her head and smiling, encouraging me to continue. I wasn't singing the lyrics, but as soon as the song started to build, Mia began twirling around. She was wearing a white sundress with long, billowing sleeves and knee-high brown boots. My little angel would have easily fit in dancing on the stage with the real band back in the seventies.

Mia could hear the music the same way I could. She had an imagination for it, and even though I was only playing the one-dimensional guitar part, I knew she could hear the full richness of the song. I watched her dance around, a picture of beauty, my soon-to-be wife, the mother of my unborn children. She closed her eyes as I built higher and higher and as soon as I hit the chorus, we both sang it at the top of our lungs.

I loved those impromptu concerts with her. We played around like that in the studio all the time, but since finding out Mia was pregnant, it's like the light that followed her around got brighter. After the morning sickness passed, she smelled better than ever before. She looked better, she glowed, her hair looked shinier, and her cheeks had a natural blush to them. It made me want to keep her pregnant for the rest of our lives. I was surprised at my own old-fashioned, primal thoughts.

When we finally stopped jamming, Mia went to grab her purse. "So, the appointment is in half an hour. Are you going with me?"

"Yep, let's go." I grabbed her hand and we headed out.

We rode the subway into the village where the OB/GYN's office was. After Mia filled out a thousand forms, the nurse took her temperature, blood pressure, and then weighed her before leading us to an exam room where she asked Mia to undress.

I stood up when a young, Asian, female doctor entered the room. "Dr. Chow," I said, reaching my hand out to greet her.

"It's Dr. Cho. Three. Simple. Letters," she said to me without cracking a smile.

"Oh, sorry, Dr. Cho. Nice to meet you."

She shook my hand, then Mia's, and then went to the sink to wash her hands.

"So, you had a positive pregnancy test at home and you're six weeks past the first day of your last menstrual cycle?" she said to Mia, who simply nodded. "Okay, then we can do an ultrasound today to confirm and see if we can

RENÉE CARLINO

find the heartbeat."

I could tell Dr. Cho was a straight shooter. She didn't mess around and probably didn't have the best bedside manner, either. She pulled the long stick from the ultrasound machine to perform the test transvaginally. Like I said, I'm a quick study. I didn't even flinch when Dr. Cho held the probe up with triumph. Mia's legs were already propped and spread in the stirrups. I stood by her head and stroked her hair while our eyes stayed glued to the monitor.

Suddenly on the screen appeared an oval shape floating in a large black circle. You could immediately see the steady flicker of a heartbeat.

There are moments in life that you know you'll never forget, even while it's happening, and that was one of them. "She's going to be a drummer!" I announced before the doctor could even speak.

Mia elbowed me. "Shhh."

That's when we heard it. It sounded like a pounding and sucking at the same time, but it was the most beautiful sound I had ever heard. It was the sound of my kid's heartbeat.

"See, baby, she's gonna be a drummer."

"What if it's a boy?" she said.

The doctor interrupted us. "We won't be able to tell the sex for some time."

"I can't imagine not having a beautiful little girl that looks just like you."

Pointing at the monitor, Mia smiled. "That's our baby."

"I know." I kissed her forehead and then swallowed

back the huge lump growing in my throat.

The doctor visit was short. She just reminded Mia to take her prenatal vitamins and then gave us a bunch of packets of information.

Back at home, lying in bed, Mia and I swept through the endless pamphlets and information booklets, periodically asking each other questions.

"Oh, look, we can tour the hospital. You're not thinking you're gonna have the baby at home, are you?"

"Martha suggested it, but I'm not crazy."

"Good. That would make me a nervous wreck."

"If it's a girl, I want to name her Grace."

"Okay, if it's a boy, I think we should name him Hamsel," I said, straight-faced.

"What?" Her tone was not nice.

"Yeah, I've always loved the name Hamsel, or we can name him Wilbur Jr. and just call him Junior for short." I finally had mercy when Mia's eyes were open as wide as they would go. "I'm kidding. What names do you like?"

"For a boy, hmm. I don't know; we'll have to think on it. I really like Birch or Branch, you know something earthy…maybe Webb." I laughed but she deadpanned, "What? I mean if you don't like those, I also really like Stream or Haze."

Oh my God, she's serious.

She tilted her head to the side, smiled, and cackled like a witch. "Ha, ha, Will. Two can play this game."

"Thank God, I thought you were serious. Shit."

She socked me in the chest. "See, it's not fun being messed with it, is it?"

"You can mess with me anytime." I grabbed myself.

"Will!" She screamed and then jumped out of bed. As she exited the room, I heard her quietly mumble, "You're a pig."

TRACK 7: Wedding Bands

T he morning of our wedding, Mia slipped out and went to Jenny's with her mom, Martha, and Sheil to get ready while I entertained the massive number of family members who'd come into town. Along with Mia's stepdad, my parents, my brother, and six of my sisters and their families flew in for the ceremony. Our plan was to have the short-but-sweet ceremony at the pier and then everyone would go back to a local restaurant for a wedding dinner. We didn't do the reception thing. I honestly didn't think Mia would feel up to that much commotion, and it would have cost us a fortune. Since Mia didn't want to go out of town after finding out she was pregnant, I reserved a suite at the Ritz-Carlton for our wedding night.

Tyler and I dressed in simple black suits and skinny ties that Jenny picked out. I couldn't resist the temptation—I had to hide a silly T-shirt under my dress shirt to give Mia a laugh. When I showed it to Tyler, he said she was going to kick me in the balls and then kill me.

"You better not reveal that T-shirt in front of any of the family members."

"They'd get a laugh, but I'm not going to. I'll save it for later for Mia."

"What did you get her for the wedding gift?"

"Dude, I bought her a fucking Steinway."

"Are you kidding me?"

"No, I had to. She saw it in a store and played it in the showroom. The entire staff gathered around to watch her. She kept her eyes closed and wept while she played "Isolde's Love Death" from *Tristan and Isolde*. She played the whole fucking thing without any sheet music. The crowd clapped and whistled. I offered to buy it on the spot; I said we could write it off, but she said absolutely not. She wouldn't let me."

"How much was it?"

"A lot."

"Dude, tell me, how much?"

"A hundred."

"A hundred what?" Tyler said in disbelief.

"A hundred fucking shillings. A hundred thousand dollars, you moron."

"You bought her a hundred-thousand-dollar piano?"

"Well, technically, Alchemy Sound Studios bought it for her, but yeah."

They'd delivered it late last night. I planned to take her there before we met everyone at the restaurant.

"Maybe you guys can do some baby-making business on there while you're at it."

I tightened my skinny tie in the long mirror nailed to our closet door, and then I turned toward Tyler. I put my hand on his shoulder. "You've been an awesome friend to me, man. I love you—that's why I don't want to lie to you."

"What?" he said, looking innocently at me.

"Mia's pregnant. We found out for sure a couple of days ago."

He gave me the biggest bear hug and lifted me off the ground in the process. "Oh, man, that's awesome news, bro."

A bear hug from Tyler truly felt like a bear hug. Being six foot myself, I was rarely picked up and twirled around by others. I was surprised by his reaction. I thought it would be upsetting to him.

"Tyler, Jen already knows. Mia told her." I'm not positive, but I thought his eyes looked a little watery after I made that comment.

He continued smiling. "Jenny will be okay. She's tough as nails, man."

"Yeah, I know."

"Anyway, it's about you guys today. I promise I won't make a huge fool out of myself like you did at my wedding."

"Hey, I was heartbroken."

We trotted down the stairs from my loft with my sisters and a bunch of kids in tow. We got to the Fulton Ferry Landing early. The day was perfect: sunny, crisp and clear. Even from the other side of the bay, all the way across the choppy water, the New York skyline was grand. I stood against the railing next to Tyler and my brother while I watched my mom and sisters chase my nieces and nephews around. I wondered what Mia would look like, how she would be feeling, and if she would make the announcement right there on the pier or if she would wait until later at the restaurant.

My brother said little to me that day until right before Mia arrived.

"Will?"

"Yeah." I turned to my brother, Ray, who was sixteen years older than me and had been married for twenty-five years. At five years old, I'd been the ring bearer in his wedding.

"I'm only going to tell you this once—it's my only advice to you." He glanced toward his wife, Michelle, who at forty-five was a striking and exotic beauty. Frankly, I didn't know what she saw in my brother after all those years. He was kind of a dick. "Always listen."

"Huh?" I said.

"That's all they want is someone to listen to them."

It was the simplest advice, but I realized something: it was the reason Michelle and Ray had been together and happy after all those years. He was attentive to her. He talked highly of her. I never once heard him complain. She was his queen and he kept her on that pedestal the same way I would with Mia.

"Thanks, Ray."

He gave me a half hug and then I felt his head jerk up to look past me. "She's beautiful, Will. Even more beautiful than I remember. Don't fuck it up, little brother."

I turned and immediately saw her. It was like all the light in the sky was funneled onto her. Everyone else looked like they were standing in a shadow. I saw her mother and Jenny and Sheil and her step-dad with Mia on his arm walking toward me. My feisty, funny girl, had found the dress. She was wearing almost an exact replica of the dress Stephanie Seymour had worn in the "November Rain" video, minus the big puffy shoulders. The front of the dress was so short it didn't hide the soft pink garter hugging her thigh. The sides and back swooped down into a short train. Seriously, people, Google the dress from "November Rain"—it's hot.

I heard Tyler whisper, "She's crazy."

"Yep," I said, grinning from ear to ear. "I fuckin' love it."

I watched her intently. All the sounds around me went away. It was quiet, but I could hear something. I strained to listen to the sound I've heard so many times before when I'm in Mia's presence. It's quiet, but if I tune everything else out, I can hear it. It's the divine sound of my soul. It's the sound I hear when I know everything is right in my world. Her dress came down low and sexy from the top and then off the shoulders. Her hair was simply pulled back into a low bun. She had no jewelry on and very natural makeup, just the delicious pink tinge to her lips that she always had. Once her eyes locked on mine, she never looked away; she came to me, right into my arms, smiling and without reluctance.

Leaning in, she whispered, "Bet you're wishing you had a red bandana right about now."

"You have no idea," I said to her. "You're the most beautiful woman I've ever seen."

"I'm a spectacle out here. Look around." She laughed. "This was all for you, baby."

The group of family members began to stir while we had our quiet exchange.

When Mia jutted her chin out to give me a peck, Tyler finally interrupted. "No! You can't do that yet."

Everyone in the group chuckled.

Tyler cleared his throat. "Family and friends, we're here today to celebrate Mia and Will and the love that they share. They've asked us to be here to witness the joy of their union."

At that point, it's fair to say that I stopped listening to Tyler. All I could think about was Mia. I saw, like in a film reel flashing in front of me, the last year of my life. I watched the heartache and the happiness and the moments of unrelenting bliss when we were in each other's arms. I thought about every mundane moment that makes up that gray area of a person's life. It's the hour or two a day that you clean your kitchen or watch TV or do the laundry. All my gray moments with Mia were colored in: chasing her around the Laundromat, spraying water on her from the kitchen sink, or messing around with her on the couch while we spent whole days watching reruns of *The Office*. I looked forward to the rest of my life, even if the rest of my life only consisted of the humdrum day-in, day-out bullshit, it didn't matter because Mia turned the most unremarkable moments into moments I cherished.

"Will?" She breathed out, her face paralyzed with terror.

"Yeah?"

"Your vows, baby. Aren't you gonna say your vows?"

Oh my God, poor Mia thought I was getting cold feet.

"Yes, my vows, okay." I cleared my throat. "Mia, you're my best friend and that's not some clichéd crap a guy says to a girl. You really are my best friend. You're funnier, smarter, and prettier than Tyler, and you smell way better." I paused as everyone laughed. "But seriously, something came alive in me the day I met you. It was so strong a force that I knew completely and with all my heart that you would be in my life forever."

Mia's eyes filled with tears. Her cheeks turned pink, her eyes grew wide, and she smiled so serenely I began to get choked up myself.

I took her hands. "Mia, I promise that I will never stop loving you, laughing with you, playing music with you, crying with you. I promise I will never stop dancing with you and cuddling you and bringing you chocolate and wine." I wiped away the tears that fell from her eyes. "I'm yours forever and I choose you to be mine."

"Will," she began in a cracked voice. "Your love is so pure and real that I can feel it in your fingertips when I touch you. I can see it in your eyes and the way you smile at me. I'm so in love with you because you are the most genuine, kind, and loving human being I have ever met." She leaned in and whispered, "And you have nice abs." We both chuckled and then she continued. "You're the smartest, coolest, and most talented guy I know. I promise that I will worship you better than any groupie ever could. I will love you, Will Ryan, until the day I die. And I will be your best friend too."

Tyler couldn't get a word in before I crushed Mia's lips with mine. The crowd clapped. We walked around hugging and kissing our family members and friends. Mia's mom cried, which was unusual for her.

Jenny had insisted on hiring a photographer to document the event. Mia and I had fun doing silly poses with all the kids, and then when it was our turn to take photos alone, we couldn't keep our hands off of each other. I dipped my head down and nuzzled my face into Mia's neck. She linked her legs between mine and we let the photographer snap away while we stood there embracing each other under the Brooklyn Bridge.

When it was time for us to leave, everyone threw birdseed at us, which was weird, but apparently it's illegal to throw rice because it chokes the birds. They gave all the little nieces and nephews the bulk of the birdseed, so you can imagine the scene as Mia and I scurried to the limo. They were throwing birdseed almost directly into our faces, so not only were we swarmed by birds overhead, but we were spitting out birdseed and wiping it out of our mouths the whole way to the car. Something always has to go wrong at a wedding, and all things considered that wasn't the worst that could have happened.

Inside the limo, I gave the driver our address.

"Why are we going back home?" Mia asked.

"I have a surprise for you."

"Well, I have a little surprise waiting for you in the studio, so I guess we might as well stop in there too."

I squeezed her hand. "Were you in there this morning, you sneaky little mouse?"

"No, why?"

"So you didn't see my present to you?"

"No, actually I gave my mom the key so she could leave my gift to you down there. I was going to give it to you tomorrow."

Before putting up the privacy screen, I told the driver to drive around for a bit and then I got on my knees in front of Mia and slowly pulled her garter off with my teeth. She opened her legs just enough for me to spot her light blue, lace panties.

"Is that superstitious or traditional?" I said to her in a low voice.

"I just thought you would like them." She shrugged. "You can ditch them if you want."

See, this is why I married this girl. The beauty of Mia's early '90s throwback dress was that I was able to very easily slide her panties down.

She patted the seat on her left. I moved and undid my fly faster than John Holmes. She reached in, took a hold of me, and started stroking.

"Mmm. You are my naughty little wife now."

She leaned in and whispered near my ear, her breath hot and minty. "I just want to fuck my husband, that's all. Can I do that now?"

Oh. My. God.

"Uh huh, sure. By all means, please do not let me slow this show down for one more minute."

She climbed onto my lap, and then a moment later, I was buried inside her. She moved slowly and sensually at first. I reached over and turned the volume up on the stereo. "Ball and Biscuit" by the White Stripes was playing.

"Did you plan this?"

She began moving faster on top of me, panting hard and whimpering. "Yes." She breathed loudly.

I braced the back of her neck and kissed her hard. "You're so fucking rad."

"Everything is rad." She cried as she tried to steady her breath. I felt it coming. I heard it coming, that part in the song, about a minute forty-five into it, which just happened to coincide perfectly with what we were feeling, the building up, the sensation of reaching that peak. Right when the guitar shredding started, I flipped Mia over on her back, across the seat. She instantly placed her heels on my shoulders. I reached down and forced the front of her thighs toward me so that I was in as far as I could go, and then with my thumb I pressed down into her and began making circles in her flesh while I drove harder and harder. She was bucking against me; her eyes were closed, her mouth open, her back arched and her neck strained. The back of her head was completely pressed hard into the seat. She was bracing herself on the door behind her.

I slowed.

"Go," she yelled. "Go," she cried. "Fuck me."

Oh my God, I get to do this all the time. I picked up my pace and then something else took over. God, if I could have crawled up inside her, I would have. The warmth I felt around my dick was flooding my entire body. Her dress was bunched under her and up around her head, but she couldn't care less. My sweet, piano-playing Mia, all sex-crazed and unashamed. Her mouth was open as far as it could go, but no sound was coming out. I watched her in wonder; all I could hear was the screeching of the electric guitar and then finally when I did hear her, it was unintelligible sounds of rapture. I was feeling some sort of delirium when it was all over with. I was as motionless as could be, on my knees, still holding her legs around me. She opened her eyes. She looked ravished, pink from the cheeks down.

"I love you," she said, looking right in my eyes.

I leaned over her and kissed her sweet mouth. "Let's never leave this limo. Let's just wither up and die here. I'll starve to death in this limo with a goddamn smile on my face." I nipped at her lip and then her neck. "You are a sexy little thing, by God."

She giggled and then something occurred to me. I can't actually say that it occurred to me, it was more like it shot me point-blank with a freakin' bazooka. It was the image of my tiny baby cocooned inside a balloon of amniotic fluid, right there in the spot that I was so cheerfully jabbing my dick into. I suddenly felt light-headed. I began to sway as I hovered over Mia.

"What's wrong?" She was squinting at me and repeating the question. "What's wrong? What's wrong, Will?"

Her voice became frantic, but I was unable to find my own. She pushed me back against the seat and leaned over me, searching my eyes. She put her hand to my cheek.

I braced her hips with my hands and looked down at her belly. Finally my voice cracked and I said, "Are you okay?"

"Of course I'm okay." She took a deep breath. "What just happened to you?"

"How can that not have hurt the baby?"

She stared into my eyes for several moments. Her demeanor changed. I could see anger boiling behind her big hazel eyes. "Jesus, Will, your neurosis is getting really out of control. It's going to start affecting your health; you have to calm down. You need to get your anxiety in check. Whatever you need to do to stop this constant catastrophizing, you should do it."

"Thanks, wife," I said sarcastically.

"I'm sorry. I just thought you were having a heart attack. I mean, you turned gray on me. I thought I had killed you with sex."

"Now who's catastrophizing?"

"I don't want to fight on our wedding day." She pressed a button, lowering the privacy screen, and then asked the driver to head to our loft.

I spoke to her in a low, defeated voice. "It just seems weird that it wouldn't hurt the baby."

She took my hand and finally her expression turned sympathetic. "The baby is tucked away in there and very safe. Your dick, although very big, honey, is nowhere close to reaching the baby." She was protecting my ego. "This is natural. You asked me to be open and honest with you, so I will. I thought once I became pregnant that the idea of sex would sound revolting, but it's actually the opposite. I'm super horny." She whispered the last part.

"Oh yeah?" My voice got high.

"Yes, and you shouldn't worry. Back in the day, people didn't even know they were pregnant at this stage. I love your concern, I do." She kissed my nose. "But you're going to kill yourself worrying like that."

"Okay," I mumbled just as the limo stopped in front of our building.

We pulled our ravaged selves together and headed into the studio. I walked behind Mia into the control room. The most gratifying feeling in the world was watching Mia's reaction when she looked through the glass and saw the Steinway.

"Holy shit," she mumbled. "You bought the Steinway."

It wasn't a question.

I stood behind her and wrapped my arms around her waist.

She immediately turned and looked up at me with the most serious look on her face. "You are so getting a blow job tonight."

This horny pregnancy thing is not so bad.

I nodded. "I'm okay with that."

"Wait a minute," she said excitedly, "You're gonna die when you see what I got you."

"I hope not."

She punched me in the arm and then grabbed my hand and pulled me along. Walking behind her, I noticed that her hair was a total mess in the back from our little limo escapade. She had taken it out of the bun and crazy pieces were going everywhere. I laughed as she led me into the sound room.

"What's so funny?"

"Your hair looks a bit...well, it looks a little..." I tried to pat the back down, but there was so much hairspray coating each strand that it wouldn't budge.

"Through good and bad, honey, remember?" she said with a coy smirk. "Anyway, you'll forget all about my hair when you see this..."

She moved away from one of the guitar stands, revealing an Ebony Les Paul. Upon further inspection, I noticed there was a signature. My eyes watered; I shook my head in disbelief. It was an electric guitar signed by Jimmy Page. I picked it up and it was like I was holding the holy mother-fuckin' grail. In twelve seconds flat, I discovered the meaning of life while holding that guitar. I turned to thank Mia and found her donning a shiny gold halo and angel wings.

"I knew it. This is heaven, right?" I said to her.

She laughed. Okay, she didn't really have wings and a halo, but she was as angelic as I had ever seen her, with her tousled hair, pink lips and white dress. It also didn't hurt that she had just bought me my eternal wet dream.

"Not that this day could get any better, but what would it take to get your glorious little ass over to that drum kit?"

Mia rarely played the drums. She didn't play them very well either, but I needed a drummer and she was the only one around. She kicked off her heels and skipped over to the stool as I plugged in my new precious baby.

"Which song?" she asked. There were plenty of good reasons why Mia didn't normally play drums. For starters, she held the sticks awkwardly. Actually, I'm being generous when I say awkwardly. She held them like they were goddamn horse reins. She sat there in her pretty dress with her legs spread, one foot on the bass drum pedal and the other one on the high hat, the picture of a complete rock star if only it didn't like look she was about to play the xylophone.

"You are so cute, baby." I grinned and she smiled and bounced on the stool giddily. "'When the Levee Breaks.'"

I watched as she searched her mind for the beat and then away she went, pounding like John fuckin' Bonham. I didn't adjust the strap, so the guitar was resting lower on my body than usual. I pushed my right leg out to play as best I could. Mia didn't let up, so neither did I. Her hair was in her face and she was sweaty, and she only looked up at me at the bridge, and then I saw some sort of disbelief in her eyes. That's what happens when you pay attention to your surroundings while you play the drums. You realize that not everyone is living in a loop. She messed up a few times and then closed her eyes and found the beat again.

I could mess up a thousand times and no one would notice, but mess up on drums and you screw everyone. Good thing it was just Mia and me that night...playing a Jimmy Page guitar, playing a Led Zeppelin song, and Jesus Christ, if that wasn't a wedding present to remember. Imagine it's thirty years from now and you're thinking back to the day you married your wife. Was she pregnant with your child, playing "When the Levee Breaks" on the drums, in a wedding dress with no underwear on because you fucked her silly in the back of a limo? Yeah, be jealous.

TRACK 8: Full Bellies, Full Hearts

I t took a lot of convincing for me to finally agree to leave the studio after our wedding ceremony. Mia didn't want the guests waiting too long at the restaurant for us. I chased her up the stairs to the loft and into our bedroom. I helped unzip her, and then I watched her change into a casual white dress. She topped it off with a black leather jacket. That's when I revealed the T-shirt I'd been hiding underneath my dress shirt.

"You are not wearing that to our wedding dinner," she said with her hand on her hip.

"Tyler said you'd kick me in the balls when you saw it."

"If you don't take that off, I will."

My T-shirt said "Buy Me a Beer, The End is Near" and then underneath the writing there was a picture of a ball and chain.

"It's a joke. This couldn't be further from how I feel."

She scrunched up her nose and gave me the pouty face.

I moved toward her, pushed her hair behind her ears, and tilted her head up to look at me. "I honestly feel like this is the beginning of my life, Mia."

"Me too," she said. "I've just been really sensitive about stuff lately."

"Why?"

"I don't know, sometimes I think it was the way you reacted when I told you I was pregnant. It made me think we were rushing into all this."

I held her face in my hands and glanced past her into the hallway where June was pooping on the hardwood floor. I didn't say anything; I focused my eyes back on Mia. "Listen to me. That kind of news is eye-opening for all men. Yes, I wondered how we would make it work and what it would mean for me to be a father, but then I remembered what Martha said to us in the café. She said we had everything we needed between us, and I think she's right."

I bent and kissed her slowly and for a long time. When I opened my eyes, hers were still closed and there were tears streaming down her cheeks. I wiped them away with my thumbs. "Baby, don't cry. It's our wedding day. We had awesome sex, we have two new, kickass instruments that are a hundred percent tax deductible, and we have a sweet little baby on the way."

She looked up finally and smiled. "I love you."

"I love you too, Mia Ryan. Doesn't that have a nice ring?"

"Yes, it does. I guess we should get to the restaurant." She pushed me away, looked down at my T-shirt, and pointed toward the closet. "Go change or my mom will disown you and probably kick you in the balls herself."

"Fine." I shuffled over to the closet and changed into a plain black T-shirt and black jeans. Mia liked it when I wore black. She would get this giddy look on her face and her cheeks would turn pink. "How's this?"

"Perfect." She giggled.

"Oh, hold on one sec. Come here, baby." I grabbed her by the shoulders and moved her to the bed to sit, facing away from the door. "Stay here, don't move."

I cleaned up June's poop in thirty seconds flat and then returned to Mia.

"What did you do?" she asked.

"Nothing. Let's hit it, pretty lady."

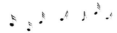

We got to Rosetta's, a small American bistro in Brooklyn that we'd rented out for the evening. When we arrived, everyone had taken good advantage of the open bar and appetizer rounds. Tyler was already slurring and Jenny looked pissed. We greeted the guests and mingled with everyone until dinner was served. Mia stood up and addressed the crowd, something extremely out of character for her. I thought for sure she expected me to make the announcement. She took my hand in hers before she started her speech.

"Thank you, everyone, for being here. Will and I feel extremely grateful for having family and friends to share this day with." She picked up her glass, raised it, and very quickly said, "I'm drinking apple cider because I'm pregnant! So cheers to family and making it bigger!"

"Cheers!" I said with the crowd and clanked my glass with Mia's.

"How was that?" she said.

"Great, honey." It may very well have been the worst wedding speech ever.

Two people immediately rushed our table—Mia's mom and Tyler. Tyler arrived first, but Liz, who only came up to Tyler's waist, stomped on his foot and then cut in front of him. She glared at us from the other side of the table.

"Mom, I was going to tell you."

Liz didn't speak; she just glared at Mia before turning to me. "You better take good care of them."

I stood up and walked around the table to hug Liz. She started to cry but tried desperately to contain it. I brought her into my chest. "I love Mia and that baby more than anything. I feel like they're a part of me. It's the boundless, from the depth of our souls kind of love, can't you see that?"

She sniffled. "The two of you remind me of her father and me when we were just starting out."

"You've got that wrong, Liz." I knew she was paranoid Mia would be like her and quickly grow tired of the musician way of life. "The reason you've got that wrong is because you assume Mia is like you." Liz was one of the most pragmatic people I knew. She was a lawyer and she handled everything in life the way she handled her cases, and although Mia had a trait like that, Mia was much more spontaneous and artistic and adventurous than Liz. Plus Mia was a musician herself. "She's like her dad too."

She stared blankly at me for several moments until I finally saw the sparkle in her eye. It was a realization. She cupped my face and nodded. "You might be right, Will. I just want her to be happy."

"We jammed for thirty minutes in the studio before we came here and it was the happiest I've ever seen her."

"Okay, I'll have to trust you."

"Trust her too. Trust her judgment. She put me through a year of torturous hell, and she trampled on my heart at least fourteen times just to make sure we were right for each other."

She laughed and I smiled—I knew that got to her. She was proud of her little girl for doing her homework. When I turned back to look at Mia, she was hugging Tyler. I had taken care of the angry mother of the bride and she was taking care of the piss-drunk and peeved best man. What a team. Mia's mom kissed both of us and tried not to cry while Mia's step-dad patted me a little too hard on the back, saying "Congratulations!" over and over again.

I found Jenny and Tyler talking quietly to each other in the corner, so I dragged Mia over to them.

"You guys okay?"

"I thought I was gonna give the speech?" Tyler slurred while sloppily hanging on Jenny's shoulder.

"I told you Tyler, you can give us your speech now. It will be more personal that way," Mia said, hoping to keep the drunk guy away from the microphone.

"I was just gonna say I love you guys."

"We love you too," Mia and I both replied

"We have some news," Jenny said quietly.

No one said a word for several moments. I glanced at

the champagne glass Jenny was holding.

"I'm drinking apple cider too," she said.

"Oh my God, you're pregnant?" Mia shouted.

"Yes," she cried.

They were both blubbering messes.

"I know this one will stick, Jenny, I just know it."

For everyone's sake, I hoped Mia was right.

We left our wedding before most of the guests. We took a cab to the Ritz, where I insisted on carrying Mia through the main door into the lobby and then again into our suite. We spent the whole night naked and tangled up in each other. Sometime before sunrise, when the delicate blue light became visible through the window, Mia whispered to me, "Why do you think people do it?"

Based on what she and I had spent the last hours doing, my answer was easy. "Because it feels good." I didn't realize she was talking about something else.

"Why do you think people get married and have children is what I mean?"

"Because it feels good." I pulled her naked little body toward me under the covers and threw my leg over her. "Doesn't this feel good?"

"Yes, but we don't have to be married to do this."

"We're married now, Mia, so I have no idea where this conversation is going, but to answer your question seriously, I think people get married because they want to share their lives with someone, because they want someone to experience life with."

"What does that mean?"

I kissed her nose and tucked her into my chest. "It means the beauty and wonder that I see in you every day colors each page of my life and makes it more vibrant. You make my experiences more meaningful."

She nuzzled her face into my neck and murmured, "You're such a cheese ball, Will, but you're going to be the best husband and dad."

And then she sank down under the covers and delivered on her promise.

TRACK 9: Cigarettes & Baby Bottles

T he next few months flew by, each week dictated by a new chapter in the pregnancy encyclopedia. The holidays were a blur of chaos in the studio and at the café. We took a few days off in December and traveled to Detroit and Ann Arbor to visit family. I learned very painfully that my fear of flying hadn't improved. Naturally, I was even more of a maniac on the plane than usual. It wasn't enough that I had to worry about myself plummeting to earth in a fiery ball of wreckage, now I had to worry about my wife and unborn child doing the same. Mia had little patience for my antics, I think because I refused to get help for it.

Mia and Jenny had become obsessed with all things baby. Jenny's pregnancy did stick and they found out they were having a girl right at the sixteen-week mark. We chose not to find out even though everyone we knew, Jenny being the worst of them all, berated us about it. She complained that our little boy or girl would only ever be dressed in green and yellow and people wouldn't know what to buy us. That was the one and only thing Mia wasn't being a total control freak about, so we stuck to our plan to not find out.

Martha would come over every week and check on Mia and work with her on relaxation and breathing exercises to prepare for the natural labor. Jenny was on board with the natural thing too, so of course she and Mia dragged Tyler and me to the Bradley Birthing Method classes.

It was hysterical; we had to get in all kinds of weird poses with the girls while they mimicked being in labor. We would massage their backs while they were perched on all fours, moaning. One of the hardest things I've ever done is contain my laughter during those classes. Mia was the freakin' teacher's pet because she was taking it so seriously.

Right around the third class, they showed us a video of a live birth. I had nightmares for a week after that. Tyler and I agreed that we had to find a way to get out of going to the classes.

We hadn't mutually agreed on a plan, so during the fifth class, Tyler took it upon himself and used his own bodily gifts to get us into a heap of trouble. Tyler is lactose intolerant, and he has to take these little white tablets every time he eats cheese. The morning of the class, he stopped by the studio with a half-eaten pizza. I didn't even think twice about it until that night in class during our visualization exercises when this god-awful, horrendous odor overtook our senses.

At first everyone kept quiet and just looked around for the source. There wasn't a sound to accompany the lethal attack, so everyone went into investigation mode, staring each other down. Mia began to gag. I heard Jenny cry a little behind us. Finally when I turned toward Tyler, I noticed he had the most triumphant glimmer in his eyes. I completely lost my shit. I was rolling around, laughing hysterically.

Mia grabbed the hood of my sweatshirt and pulled me to my feet. "Outside, now!" She was scowling as she dragged me along. When we passed Tyler, she pointed to him angrily. "You too, joker."

Mia and Jenny pressed us up against the brick wall outside and then gave us the death stare, both of them with their arms crossed over their blooming bellies. They whispered something to each other and then turned and walked off, arm in arm.

We followed. "Come on, you guys, it was funny."

Jenny stopped dead in her tracks and turned. She jabbed her index finger into my chest and said, "Yes, it is funny. *When you're five!* Not when you're in a room full of pregnant women. Do you know how sensitive our noses are?"

I shrugged. "It wasn't me."

"Oh, I know he's a child," she said but wouldn't even look at Tyler. "And you are too, Will, for encouraging it."

Mia was glaring at me with a disappointed look, and then she shook her head and turned to continue down the street. Jenny caught up and walked away with her.

"God, they're so sensitive," I whispered to Tyler.

"Yeah, I kinda feel bad."

Without turning around, Mia yelled to us, "You guys don't have to come anymore. Jenny and I can be each other's partners."

I turned to Tyler and mouthed, "It worked!" I had a huge smile on my face.

Tyler and I high-fived.

"Why don't you guys go celebrate? I know that's what you wanted," Jenny yelled back as they made a sharp turn down the sidewalk and down the stairs to the subway.

"Nothing gets past them," Tyler said.

When Tyler and I finally made it to the platform, Mia was gone.

"Where's Mia?" I said to Jenny, who was trying to ignore me.

She stared straight forward but still answered me. "She caught the subway going that way." She pointed. "To Brooklyn, to your home. It was just about to go—the doors were closing when we got down here."

"And you let her get on by herself? She's fucking pregnant, Jenny."

"I'm well aware. She's a big girl; she can ride the subway alone once in a while."

I started pacing, my heart pounding. Tyler just looked like a clueless oaf standing there, waiting for someone to tell him what to do. Jenny leaned against a pole and played on her phone. I took off and ran to the other side of the station to catch the train I needed to be on. Tyler yelled at me to wait, but I ignored him. I rode the subway back to Brooklyn and ran into a liquor store, bought a pack of cigarettes, and then continued the block and half back to my building. I skipped every other stair up to our loft and flew through the door. Mia wasn't home. *Fuck, oh fuck, oh fuck.*

I called her from my cell but she didn't pick up. I

texted her and then left a voice mail. I was almost in tears. "Please, baby, tell me you guys are okay." Weeks before, I had started referring to Mia and the baby as you guys. "I'm a nervous wreck."

Standing in front of our building, I lit a cigarette and nervously sucked and puffed it. I was down to the filter in one minute flat. I pulled another cigarette out and did the same. Finally, I spotted her, strolling down the street toward me, accompanied by Tyler.

"What the fuck?" I yelled when they were still a block away.

Tyler walked Mia to the end of the block and then threw his hand up, waving good-bye. I didn't wave back. When Mia reached me, I was shaking my head. "What, you were hiding behind a fucking pole, waiting for me to lose it and go running after you?"

Never breaking a smile, she stood there with her arms crossed. "We didn't think you would take off."

"I was going after you, my wife, my pregnant wife. Did you think that was funny?"

"I thought it was about as funny as a grown man intentionally farting in a birthing-method class."

"That wasn't me!" I shouted.

"But you laughed."

"Why is everyone mad at me and Tyler just gets off scot-free?"

"Oh, he'll get his turn, trust me. There's nothing quite like the wrath of Jenny—you know that."

I looked down at Mia's waist. Her tiny belly was poking through her coat. "It's freezing out here. Let's get you inside. I'm sorry about tonight, okay?"

"I just want you to take this natural-birth thing seriously with me, Will. It's going to be a big deal. I need to be prepared and I need you on my team. Jenny's due date is a month and half after mine. I'm going to have to do this first. I want this so bad, but I'm already doubting myself."

"Okay, I need to get you guys inside." I wrapped my arm around her waist and rubbed her belly as we climbed the stairs.

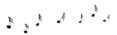

Most of our time was occupied with the scouring of baby magazines, books, and stores for all the right items. Martha had a small baby shower for Mia and Jenny at the café. We got boppies and bottles and booms and bam bams and bassinets and boo boos and bonnets and binkies and all that fucking crap we probably didn't need.

The studio efforts had been running smoothly until one evening when I got a phone call from Charlie. She said Chad was having some problems with the label. She asked if I could get Frank and have a sit-down with Michael and Chad. Apparently the label was going to request a meeting to discuss the album in its current state, and Michael and Chad wanted us to be prepared.

Our meeting was scheduled early on a Saturday morning in February. I let Mia sleep in, but I left her a note on her teakettle like I always did. That morning I wrote: **YOU ROCK ME LIKE A HURRICANE.**

Mia had a hefty collection of notes that I had left her; she kept them in a jar on the counter. I told her I didn't want to be one of those couples who texted each other from the other room. Each morning that I got up before her, which was many once she became pregnant, I would leave her a sticky note. I tried to keep it original. Sometimes the note would just say **HI** or **MAY THE FORCE BE WITH YOU** or **I LOVE YOUR BUNS. WINK.** She always found a creative way to thank me.

When I got to the studio, I opened the conference room and put some coffee on. Frank, Michael, and Chad arrived shortly after. We greeted each other and took our seats. When Chad smiled at me, I noticed that he looked older, more mature. There was something tired about his expression; he almost looked defeated.

"All right, what's up, guys?"

Michael came right out and said it. "They're not happy with the album in its current state and they want to postpone the release."

"Are you guys happy with the album?" I asked.

Before they could answer, Frank interjected. "Wait a minute. What aspect of the album are they not happy with?"

"They said they want a ballad, a love song, and a hit with a hook. Apparently you guys haven't delivered on that."

"'Lost N Found' is your ballad and 'Soldier' is your hit," I said.

"It's not commercial enough, that's what they're saying. You know this Bieber kid is writing songs directly to the audience. He's a superstar and that's what they want for Chad," Michael said.

I could feel the anger boiling behind my eyes. "First of

all, Chad is not thirteen years old. I was trying to produce an album that would get him some attention as a singer, not as a teen heartthrob." I turned to address Chad directly. "I mean, is this what you want, man?" When he just shrugged, I said, "Well, you better polish your dance moves because that's what you'll be doing on stage, dancing and lip-syncing."

Frank sat quietly until finally he reminded me of why I had hired him back in the days when I was starting out. "Let me talk to you all for a second." He took off his fedora and set it on the table, clasped his hands together, and leaned in. "I've been at this game for a while. We're witnessing a huge shift occur in the music industry. The record labels are dying because the record is dying. When someone likes a song, they can download it for a dollar or steal a bootlegged copy for free online. You don't even have to buy the rest of the album—that's why there is so much pressure for an artist to have multiple hits on one album. Look around; record stores are closing because it's all going digital. Think of it like this: when was last time you bought a roll of film? See any photo labs around? It's happening very quickly with music and books too. No more record stores and no more bookstores means what? It means no more labels and no more publishers. Do you think those companies will let that happen without putting up a fight? No, they'll find a way to tap into this digital market. They've given you a nice advance, but you'll never see any royalties, trust me. Ninety-nine percent of your sales will be digital, but they'll still charge you twelve pennies on every dollar for packaging. What packaging? They'll find a way to keep you under their thumb, kid. You could sell five million albums, pay your three-hundred-thousand-dollar advance back, and you still won't see another dollar. They will nickel-and-dime you on everything, including this studio time. They're sending you back to us and saying they're unhappy? That means they can take out twice as much money in studio costs. They're going to spend an inordinate amount of money to make you sound like the male version of Katy Perry. Your pride will be nonexistent. You'll owe them after everything is said and done, and then you'll get finagled into another deal. They'll probably even insist that you get veneers for that crooked tooth, and then they'll make you pay for it."

He chuckled, but the room was completely silent. His laugh echoed off the walls in a terrifying way before he took a deep breath and continued. "In the beginning, they wanted you to feel like your talent was real so you'd agree to sign your life away for the prestige of being signed with a major label. Now that they have you, they'll try to make you feel like crap until you give them what they want. These days, people need to see the musician on TV. No one listens to the radio anymore, and the people that do will buy albums from independents and small labels. So they need the whole package, and they only make money on the artists who reach celebrity status. I think they agreed to let you come to Will, knowing he wouldn't produce the crap they want, that way they could put the responsibility back on you. They didn't know who you were as an artist. They just knew you were good-looking with a good voice."

"I can't get out of my contract." Chad finally spoke. His voice was shaky.

"There are other things we can do." Frank turned to

me. "Remember the time you said you wanted people to be in awe while you performed, not because of the pyrotechnics going off on stage but because they connected to the music?" When I nodded, he said, "I have a suggestion."

I was getting worried about where the conversation was going.

"This is totally off the record." Frank leaned in farther. "Your auntie did a few good things for you, kid." Chad's face lightened and Frank said, "There is nothing in this contract that says you can't start performing these songs. That's the first good thing she did, the second was that she insisted you stick with Will." He turned to me. "How much does this mean to you?"

"Me? Not very much, if I'm being honest, Frank. I'll get my money no matter what happens to Chad."

Chad and Michael remained quiet while Frank slowly shook his head back and forth with a look of pure disappointment on his face.

"I have a baby on the way," I pleaded.

"You really just want to give up on Chad and roll over for these dummies?"

"I don't even know what you're suggesting."

"I'm suggesting that Michael and Chad go back to the label and tell them that pushing the release is fine. Tell them they'll get their ballad and hit. Meanwhile, Chad will start performing up and down the East Coast as part of the Will Ryan Band. You can promote yourselves online and gather a following. People will get to know Chad and get to know the way 'Soldier' was written. That song could be an anthem, it has a hook, but the label is right—it's not commercial, it's original."

"I can't leave Mia and go on the road while she's pregnant."

"Hold on a minute, Frank." Michael finally found his voice. "Are you saying that we leave the album as is and that Chad starts performing the songs under a different name?"

"Legally, we can make it happen. Will, get Mia down here. I'm not suggesting you leave her. We need her. I'm suggesting you both go."

"I don't think she'll be into it," I said.

"Let's see what she has to say." He motioned for me to pick up the phone and call her.

I grabbed my cell phone and texted her: **ARE YOU BUSY?**

JUST TAKING THIS PHOTO TO SAY THANK YOU. She sent me a photo of her naked from the waist up, wearing all my Post-it notes like a bikini top.

I replied, **I LOVE IT! CAN YOU GET DOWN HERE? WE NEED YOU. PUT ON A SHIRT FIRST.**

Everyone filled their coffee mugs and waited for Mia to come down. When she came in, she smiled and said hello and then took a seat at the table. Frank, in his typical fast-talking fashion, basically laid down the whole situation for Mia. At the end of a very long speech, he said, "What do you think, sweetheart?"

She looked at me first. I didn't give her any indication of how I was feeling. The truth was that it sounded interesting to me. We could do some live shows together and then during the week go back into the studio and work.

"Come May, I won't want to go too far from home."

I nodded. Her voice seemed small. She was looking for my approval, but I wanted her opinion.

"What do you think of Chad?" I asked her.

"I think he's a great singer," she said immediately. "I think the music we wrote for him gives him way more credibility. I can teach him how to get by on the piano. I wouldn't want to see the label turn him into a brand so quickly either."

"So you'll do it?" Frank said.

"Yes."

He stood up and placed his fedora on his head and said, "I'll get you guys some bookings. Will, you need to find a drummer."

He left the room and it seemed all problems were solved.

"So, I guess this means we're a band," Chad said with a goofy grin.

We had our work cut out for us.

TRACK 10: The Way It Is

M ia continued going to the birthing-method classes with Jenny while I worked with Chad in the studio, preparing for the upcoming shows Frank had booked for us. We had to keep things quiet with the label, so I had to find people I trusted. I hired Dustin, a drummer from the band I used to be in. I hadn't talked to him for a long time after he hopped in bed with my then-girlfriend, Audrey. I got over it quickly, though, when it occurred to me that she had fucked him right back. I never had to worry about stuff like that with Mia. Anyway, Dustin hated the record labels, so he posed no real threat. He was on board for the shows in a heartbeat.

We played around town mostly and Boston a lot, anywhere with a music scene that was in driving distance. Mia enjoyed the shows even though her growing belly was making playing more and more uncomfortable. Chad sang well; he had a good stage presence. I noticed within a few weeks people started coming up to us at the end of the shows. We had a pretty decent following for our tiny tour.

As time went on, we noticed that when we played the song "Soldier," which had a very catchy and loud chorus, the crowds would sing along to it. We'd played about three shows a week for five weeks before the label caught wind of our little plan.

They couldn't technically put a stop to it, but they moved Chad's release date up. They wanted to get the single for "Soldier" out before bootlegged copies from our shows were floating all over the Internet. Frank's plan had worked. Chad had his own original sound, thanks to us. I made peace with giving him the music, and by the end of the five weeks, I actually liked the kid. He was a quick study. Mia taught him some basics on the piano, and by the end of our shows, he was coming up with new music.

We all parted ways amicably. Frank moved on to look for the next big thing. I went to work with new musicians in the studio, and Mia went back to her obsession with being pregnant.

"I'm as big as a house," she said one night into the mirror above our dresser as she examined her naked body from every angle.

I watched her from the bed where I was propped against the headboard. I looked down at my own stomach and noticed it was a bit harder to see those ripples Tyler had so blatantly observed. I might have put on a few pregnancy pounds myself.

You couldn't tell Mia was pregnant from behind—she still had a perfect little ass—but man, when she turned, watch out. Once she reached thirty weeks into the pregnancy, her belly stuck out at least two feet from her body.

"You're not big, you're beautiful."

"I'm a cow. I'll never be sexy again."

"Turn around, Mia, so you can see just how sexy I think you are."

Mia's boobs and belly had gotten huge, but she was just as beautiful as before, if not more. Her skin was shiny and vibrant and pink and lush. As she turned, I quickly slipped out of my boxers and threw them aside.

She scanned my body up and down and then her face morphed into the pity-party face. "Are you thinking about someone else?" She actually started crying.

Fuck. "In the name of all that is good and holy, Mia, you are standing in front of me naked. I'm turned on because of you."

"How can you want me like this?" She sniffled.

"Come on, stop that." I motioned for her to get on top of me. "Climb aboard, baby, let's have some fun."

She brushed her hair out of her face and climbed up onto the bed. She straddled me and then bent to kiss me, but I could tell it was uncomfortable for her to bend over her belly. Leaning back with a sad look on her face, she took hold of me and then sat up on her knees to guide me inside her. I felt a tear hit my stomach. She was still crying.

"No, stop, baby. Don't do that." I pulled her onto the bed next to me. "Lie on your side so you're comfortable, sweet thing." I climbed over her and looked at her face. "You gonna be okay?"

She nodded unconvincingly, but I proceeded to kiss her all over anyway. I kissed her belly and sang to her and sang to my baby. Ray LaMontagne's "Shelter" was blaring from the iPod dock. I sang along to it like I had written it just for her. After ten minutes, Mia started moving with me, kissing me and answering each touch.

I curled up behind her and pulled her leg back over mine and then I made love to her on her side. I kissed and sucked at her neck. She whimpered.

"Do you see how beautiful you are to me?" I said near her ear. Pushing her head back against my shoulder, I watched as she opened her mouth, closed her eyes, and found that happy place. I held her against my chest, one arm gripping her leg and the other holding her around the shoulders as I continued my slow and deliberate movements against her. The tension in her body was gone. We moved with ease and comfort until we were both sated, and then I kissed her shoulders and back as the rest of the album played out. We stayed like that, connected, with my face buried in her sweet-smelling hair until we were asleep.

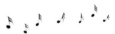

"Good morning, handsome." Mia, fully dressed and ready for the day, was leaning over me and smiling.

I squinted up at her. "Hi, pretty baby."

"Do you want to come to my prenatal appointment with me?"

"Absolutely."

Even though I generally despised being in any sort of medical building, I loved going to the prenatal visits. It was like Christmas when the doctor would put the fetal Doppler to Mia's belly. The swooshing and thumping of our baby's heartbeat was the most beautiful music Mia and I had made so far.

We got out of the loft early. Mia had on a gray baby-doll dress, black tights, boots, and a purple scarf. I wore my token hoodie and jeans. It was warming up in the city, and we both marveled at how clear and sunny the sky was.

When we got to Dr. Cho's, Mia had to do all the initial business: pee test, blood pressure, temperature, and then we were directed into the exam room. Mia undressed from the waist down, hopped up on the table, and covered herself with one of those paper blankets.

The doctor came in, flashed me a cursory smile, and said, "Mr. Ryan."

"Dr. Cho," I shot back in a completely monotone voice. You know those people who show zero emotion—there's no movement in their face or inflection in their voice? That was Dr. Cho. Saying she was robotic would be putting it mildly. She was like a robot from the eighties, completely one-dimensional and glitchy.

She lifted Mia's shirt and wrapped the measuring tape around her belly. After measuring her, Dr. Cho pressed one hand at the base of Mia's belly and the other on the top, just below her breasts.

"Hmm," she said, but nothing changed on her face. She didn't move for several moments. *Ha, another glitch.*

"Hello?" I said.

She didn't look at me; her eyes stayed focused on Mia's stomach. "Mia, I think we need to do an ultrasound."

There was still no change in her facial expression, but I knew hidden behind her statement was worry, and I could see the worry spreading to Mia as well.

"I'll be back in a minute."

Once she was out of the room, Mia let out a huge breath and then her nose scrunched into the expression she makes right before she cries.

I got about five inches from her face and said, "What did she mean, Mia?" My voice was high.

"I don't know," she said, looking anxious. I stood and started pacing. The walls were closing in. I put my hand to my head; I was burning up. I walked to the counter and started fumbling frantically through all the medical devices.

"What are you doing, Will? You're not supposed to touch that stuff."

"I have to take my temperature. Mia, this is bad news, don't you see?" I found the electronic thermometer. I placed one of those disposable plastic thingies over it and shoved the probe under my tongue.

Mia stayed on the table and glared at me. "Calm down!" She tried to whisper but it came out in a low, deep mumble. She sounded like Satan.

I started getting dizzy. The thermometer beeped. My temp was ninety-nine point zero degrees. I had a fever. When I went to dispose of the plastic sheathing, the toxic-waste receptacle wouldn't open from the foot pedal. I had to use my hand. *God, why me?* The room began spinning and suddenly all the germs that had ever been exposed in that environment became visible as tiny floating specks on the walls. In my head I was chanting hepatitis, rotavirus, tetanus, psittacosis, influenza, salmonella, cholera, botulism, anthrax.

"I have to get out of here," I whispered, out of breath.

As soon as I turned around, robot doctor was in my face. "Sit down, Mr. Ryan. Everything is going to be fine." She was wheeling in the ultrasound machine.

I sat back in a chair and tried to calm my breathing. I looked at Mia; she was shaking her head at me. It wasn't disappointment on her face—it was anger. Her eyes got smaller and beady and then she growled. I'm not exaggerating; she actually fucking growled at me.

Her entire stomach moved; something jutted out from one side, pressing against the inside of her belly like a giant alien baby trying to get out. Mia was saying something but I couldn't hear her, I could only see her mouth moving in slow motion.

I blinked, trying desperately to clear my vision. Dr. Cho began squirting the clear gel on Mia's stomach. My head felt heavy as I started to sway back and forth. A black haze began filling my vision from the outside in. Mia looked at the doctor and pointed to the tongue depressors on the counter. Dr. Cho handed her one, and then Mia's chin jutted out, and she flicked her arm back and threw the damn thing right at my face. It hit my nose with a thwack and fell to the floor. Suddenly all my senses were back.

"Breathe!" she yelled.

I gasped for air; my eyes were about to pop out of my head. You would have thought I had just run a marathon by the way I was breathing. I finally calmed and stood up on shaky legs. Dr. Cho still had no expression on her face even though I'd nearly passed out in front of her.

Mia was looking at the monitor. The ultrasound machine was on and squiggly lines were dancing across the screen. Moving sluggishly toward the exam table, I took her hand in mine and began to rub the back of it. We both watched in awe as our baby appeared before our eyes.

When Mia finally looked back at me, I mouthed, "I'm sorry," but she wasn't angry anymore, she was touched.

Dr. Cho moved the ultrasound transducer across Mia's belly and then pointed to the screen. "See here." When we both nodded enthusiastically, she said, "He's still breech. That's his head at the top."

"He?" Mia and I said in unison.

That has to be the biggest rookie mistake. Blowing it for the first-time parents who want the sex of their child to be a surprise should be illegal. Doctors and technicians should be fined for that. Yeah, I know doctors are only human, but I'm only human too and I was fined for public intoxication. I didn't hurt anybody; I didn't spoil one of the only true surprises in life for two excited parents just starting out. I'd entertained people on the corner that night, but still I was arrested and fined.

Dr. Cho looked pale with a greenish tint. Robot doctor finally turned human. That's what it takes sometimes, a brutally humbling experience. She placed her hand over her mouth as her eyes grew wider with shock.

I guess fining her would be a little extreme. I had a feeling it would be the first and last time she'd burn the turkey.

"I'm so sorry," she murmured through her cupped hand.

I shook my head at her. Mia's was turned away from me, still gazing at the monitor. I leaned over and noticed that she was crying.

She looked up me and smiled. "I want to name him

Allen," she squeaked as tears dripped from her chin.

I bent and kissed her and then goddammit, I started crying too. "Yes, baby, we can name him Allen."

That was Mia's late father's name. Allen Kelly was a guy I wished I'd known. Every time I was at the café Mia had inherited from him, someone would bring up his name. He was admired in the neighborhood and greatly missed. Known as a truly free spirit who had done right by the people he loved, Allen's memory would live on in our son. I said the words "our son" to myself as I watched him suck his thumb, cozy and safe inside Mia's belly.

"So his head is up still?" Mia asked.

"Yes," Dr. Cho replied simply.

"What does that mean?" I said.

"I don't deliver breech babies vaginally. It means that Mia will have to have a C-section or find another doctor."

Mia's stare was determined. "What about an ECV?" she said as if she were a medical doctor herself.

"What's an ECV? That sounds dangerous!"

"It's a procedure to turn the baby and it sounds dangerous because it is. There is a much higher risk with that than scheduling a C-section."

"I don't want a C-section." Mia looked so shattered. "Is there any way he'll turn on his own?"

Dr. Cho's face was sympathetic, something I didn't think was possible. "It's unlikely at this stage. My recommendation is to go ahead and schedule your cesarean section for the thirty-eighth week. You'll be full term and the baby won't likely come before then. I'm very sorry," she said and then left the room.

Mia put her tights and boots back on without looking

at me. She was quiet, inside her head.

"Talk to me." I said.

She looked up, right into my eyes, and then lost it. She moved toward me quickly and buried her head in my chest. I wrapped my arms around her as she began releasing heavy sobs.

I rubbed her back and tried to soothe her. "Shh, baby. Everything is going to be okay. It doesn't matter how that baby gets to us. We should be happy he's okay."

"Mm hmm. I know."

"He didn't want to turn." I lightened my tone and she laughed a little through tears. "Lazy little fucker," I said finally.

She looked up at me. "I can't believe everything I've done to prepare for this and I don't even get to try."

"You're the toughest girl I know. You would have succeeded."

"You think so?"

She looked like a defeated child in that moment.

"Yeah, I do. Let's get outta here and go for a walk."

We found one of our favorite streets to stroll down and window-shop. I got excited thinking about having a little boy.

"Drums, I'm gonna get him on the drums first, then piano," I said to Mia excitedly as I walked backward up the street in front of her.

Her mood started to lighten as the reality set in. We were going to have a boy.

"Oh my God, Will, isn't that the cutest?" Mia stopped when something caught her eye in a store window.

It was a grey newsboy hat for a baby and a matching

one for a dad. I wrapped my arms around her from behind and swayed back and forth.

"That would look adorable on you two," she said. "I'm coming back tomorrow when they're open and buying that. You'll wear it, won't you?" she pleaded. The color and life had returned to her cheeks.

"Of course, baby."

I pulled her along and across the street. "Let's get a cab—I want to get you home and into bed."

"Hey, wait, I think that's Lauren," Mia said. She picked up her pace and began walking briskly. I followed but let her go ahead of me a few strides. "Oh my God, it is. I have to go talk to her, Will."

I recognized Lauren and knew Mia had formed some kind of special bond with her. She believed that Lauren had helped open her eyes during our time apart. Whatever Lauren had done or said, it stopped Mia from treating my heart like a pincushion. I saw a taxi headed our way, so I flagged it down and asked him to wait as I watched Mia approach Lauren. They talked and hugged as I looked on with curiosity.

When Mia finally turned around and headed toward me, she had a little bounce in her step. Leaning up on her toes, she whispered in my ear, "It's all because of her."

I looked past Mia to Lauren, who was smiling. I smiled back, blew her a kiss, and mouthed, "Good-bye, Lauren, you sweet thing."

We slid into the back of the cab. Mia shouted our address to the cabbie and then snuggled into a ball next to me.

"What did she say to you?"

"She said congratulations."

"That's it?"

"She said something like listen to the music because the answers are there."

I laughed. "Oh my God, it's Martha in the making."

Mia laughed with me. "She's older, Will. She has kids. She's been through all this. I think she was just reminding me to stay true to myself."

Squeezing her hand, I bent over to speak to my son. "Hey, man, be good to your mommy and turn over." I kissed her belly and looked up to see her expression.

With a smile barely touching the corner of her mouth, she said, "Do you want to go into the studio and mess around for a bit?"

She was trying to get her mind off the disappointing news from the doctor. Apparently the answers were in the music.

"Ooh, that's sounds hot."

"I meant musically."

"Yeah, I know," I said, but I had other plans for her.

TRACK 11: One Last Hoorah

"**W**e have an idea," I said, as Tyler and I stood in front of our very pregnant wives.

They were sitting on the couch in our loft, looking up at us skeptically with their arms crossed over their plump bellies.

Tyler waved his giant arms around. "Just hear us out."

Jenny looked away and rolled her eyes.

"We're listening," Mia said.

I addressed Mia first. "Okay, you and I know the exact date that our baby will be born, and Jenny is not due for another month and a half, so…"

"Spit it out!" Jenny snapped.

I put on the most serious face I could muster. "We're about to embark on a journey." I used the *Twilight Zone* voice. "Full of involuntary sleepless nights, throw-up, and out-of-control behavior. Our freedom will no longer exist; our identities will vanish before our very eyes. We. Will. Be. PARENTS!" I mimicked loud, thundering music.

"Glad you're excited," Mia said.

"What's the one thing we should do before that becomes a reality?" Tyler asked.

I waited.

Mia looked at Jenny and shrugged. "Take out a life insurance policy?"

"Eeehh." Tyler made a buzzer sound.

Jenny said, "Come on, you guys. Let's be honest, Mia and I are already parents." She held her hands out, gesturing toward Tyler and me. "This is about you guys. Cut to the chase."

I pointed my index finger right at Jenny's face and said, "Bingo! We want to go to the Hamptons and get fucked up and then go stay at your uncle's cottage."

Tyler chimed in, "We're inviting you guys because we need a designated driver." I elbowed him and whispered without moving my mouth, "Shut up, man."

Mia just shook her head and looked disappointed, but Jenny looked different, she had fury behind her eyes. She stood up and put her hands on her hips. "You two kill me."

I interrupted and tried to do some damage control. "Jenny, listen to me. We thought you and Mia would enjoy the cottage. You can relax in the sun overlooking the pond all day Saturday while Tyler and I wait on you two hand and foot. We'll cook and we'll clean—all you have to do is sit there and talk about diaper-rash cream and nipple confusion and whatever mumbo jumbo you two come up with." I said the next part really fast and low. "And then we'll go out Saturday night and have some fun."

A smile started forming on her mouth. She laughed. "You mean you guys will have some fun while we drive your drunk asses around?"

"I'm fine with it," Mia murmured from the couch.

Jenny turned around, shocked. "What?"

"I'm too tired to care," Mia said. "We can't drink, but they can, so why should we stop them?" *I like her more and more every day.* "We'll do this for them and then they'll owe us until the end of time." She smiled triumphantly. *I spoke too soon.*

Jenny waddled toward the door. "Fine!" she said without turning around. "Let's go, Tyler. We'll see you guys Saturday."

Tyler and I delivered on our promise to basically cater to Jenny and Mia all day Saturday at the cottage; neither one of them made it easy on us. At lunchtime Tyler was going to make sandwiches, but Mia said she was craving fish tacos and Jenny wanted a gyro.

"Come on, ladies, let's be reasonable," I said to them as they sat in lounge chairs overlooking the small pond.

Mia looked up and batted her eyelashes at me. "But it's what we want, Wilbur."

We drove all over the Hamptons looking for gyros and fish tacos and salted caramels and Sour Patch Kids.

When we returned with all the items requested, Jenny said, "Now I'm craving a burger."

We drove to a beachside restaurant and bar, where after a day of being servants, Tyler and I decided it was time. We went straight to whiskey, no wine, no beer, not even a vodka martini; it was whiskey time. Jenny and Mia sat out on the heated patio overlooking the beach where Jenny finally got her burger. Mia ordered a hot-fudge sundae for dinner. She'd been the picture of pregnancy health until she found out she was having a C-section. After that, it was a free-for-all. One night I'd watched her eat an entire family-sized bag of powdered donut gems in one sitting. She was still tiny compared to most, but I think there was some resignation in her that wasn't there before. She knew certain outcomes were out of her control, so she made the best of her final weeks of pregnancy.

I wasn't sure how much time went by, I could only measure in drinks. About five drinks in, I climbed up on the bar and addressed the crowd. I could see Mia and Jenny through the window. They were watching me... and they were mortified.

"I just want to make an announcement," I slurred. No one tried to stop me, not even the bartender. "I'm about to become a father."

The crowd cheered as I held up my drink. Mia came in and leaned against the inside of the door to watch me.

"My beautiful wife"—I gestured toward her and as everyone looked on, I saw people's faces light up when they saw her belly—"is giving me a son. I want to share a prayer with you. It's a prayer for us, all three of us." Pulling a piece of paper from my pocket, I glanced at Mia and thought I could see a smile touching the corners of her mouth.

However many miles,
We'll travel them together.
However many sunsets,
We'll watch in awe together.
We'll play our songs...
We'll laugh to tears...
We'll cry our sorrows...
And we'll face our fears... together.
The three of us.

"Drinks for everyone," I shouted.

The bar erupted. When I looked over to the door, Mia was gone. I downed two more drinks and then found Tyler first. He was wasted and I wasn't far behind.

"Did you see where Mia and Jenny went?"

"Yeah, dude, Mia doesn't feel good. They went to the bathroom."

I wish I could say that statement sobered me up, but I was beyond words being of any help.

I stumbled to the women's bathroom and pressed my head to the door. "Mia, are you okay?"

Jenny yelled back, "I think we have to go."

I pushed the door open and went inside. The other women in the bathroom all scattered except for Jenny. Mia was leaning over the sink, splashing cold water on her face.

"Baby, what's wrong?"

She turned to me, holding her stomach, but before she could speak, she buckled over and sucked air through her teeth like she was in pain. "I think it's just false labor," she finally said. "I've been having those Braxton Hicks contractions lately. I think that's what it is."

"What if it's not? I have to get you to the hospital."

"You're in no condition to drive, Will," Jenny said.

"No shit, Jenny, you're going to drive us. We're all going. Let's go get Tyler."

We had brought Jenny's dad's Lexus sedan, which had a GPS, thank God. We were able to locate all the hospitals on the way. Mia insisted we head for New York Methodist where she planned to have little Allen. She said if it was real labor, based on the time between contractions, she thought we could make it. According to the GPS, the hospital was an hour and forty-five minutes away. We all piled in the car and took off. Jenny drove like a maniac to get us on to the main highway. Mia continued having regular contractions, and each time she would yell at Jenny to slow down.

Half an hour into it, Mia's pain became progressively worse. She started moaning through every contraction. I had her get on her hands and knees across the back seat and rock back and forth. I felt so bad for her and bad that Tyler and I had been so selfish as to think going to the Hamptons was a good idea. At the point when we were an hour away, I called Dr. Cho.

"Dr. Cho, I think Mia is in labor."

"I am in labor!" Mia yelled.

"How long has she been having contractions?"

"I don't know, about an hour." My voice was shaky.

"Calm down, Mr. Ryan. She's probably very early in her labor. Average first labors take about twelve to fifteen hours. Just relax, go to the hospital, and let the nurses check her. I'll head in there and have them prep the OR."

"Okay," I said and hung up.

"What did she say?" Everyone in the car yelled at the same time.

"She said it's probably very early in her labor."

"What?" Mia shouted. "It can't get worse. I don't think I can take it if it gets worse," she whined.

I immediately texted Martha to meet us at the hospital.

There was a moment of calm between contractions where I took Mia in my arms in the back seat. Our position was awkward, but I could tell by the way she let all her muscles go lax that she was already exhausted.

"No, no, no," she cried. "Another one is coming," she mumbled and then she was back on her knees again.

Jenny continually glanced in the rearview mirror while she gave Mia instructions. "In through your nose and out through your mouth, Mia. Make sure you pay attention to your breath."

Tyler stayed relatively quiet the whole miserable ride while Mia writhed around in the back seat of that car. I made silent prayers to any god and every god that Mia wouldn't give birth in the back seat of Jenny's dad's Lexus for no other reason except that I would have to deliver our baby. She spent time on her knees, on her back, on her side, and in every other possible position she could get into.

It got horrendously worse when we were about fifteen minutes from the hospital. The contractions were coming one on top of the other. Mia was out of her mind, moaning and yelling and sometimes just making low, guttural sounds. At one point she tried to take off her clothes, but I knew if I let her go there, out would come baby.

We pulled into the ER entrance driveway because it was after hours and the main entrance to the hospital was closed. Jenny pulled to the curb.

"Ahhh!" Mia cried. "Hurry! I can't walk—it's coming."

"Tyler, go grab a wheelchair!" I yelled.

Jenny tried to soothe Mia with words. "Visualize your body opening like a lotus flower."

"Shut the fuck up, Jenny!" Mia screamed at the top of her lungs.

Jenny looked back at me with her eyes wide.

I shook my head. I had no idea what to do besides get Mia into that hospital.

Honking sounds started coming from the rear of the car. I got out to see what the commotion was. It's safe to say I was sober when we reached the hospital, but unfortunately neither Tyler nor myself were any less belligerent.

When I got out, I saw a huge yellow Hummer behind us. The massive truck couldn't maneuver around Jenny's car, so the driver sat there and honked.

Standing next to our rear passenger door, I looked at the guy and then pointed inside the Lexus and yelled, "My wife is in labor. We're getting a wheelchair—can you hold on one second?"

"Just ignore him!" Mia barked.

The man honked again. I walked over to his window. He rolled it down and the imbecile said, "Are you gonna move or what? I need to get out of here. I made a wrong turn."

"Maybe you didn't hear when I said that my wife is in

labor in that car. She can't walk; we're getting her a wheelchair."

"Why should I care?" he said, glaring at me.

"Well fuck you very much!" I turned to walk back to our car.

The moment I crossed in front of his truck, he honked and laid on the horn for several seconds. I stopped. I could feel rage coursing through my veins. I watched Tyler roll the wheelchair to the car and then walk toward me.

In an eerily calm voice, I said, "Tyler, tell Jenny to take Mia in. I'll be in there in two minutes after I kill this fuckstick." I jutted my thumb back in the idiot's direction.

Tyler, still severely drunk, clapped his hands and said, "Let's do this."

I'm not proud of it, okay. A lot of things were running though my head. I was moments away from sending my wife into surgery and moments away from becoming a father. My life would never be the same. That's not an excuse, because if anything that would be the time to become a law-abiding citizen. I wasn't thinking straight.

I walked to the guy's door, very casually opened it, reached up, and pulled the idiot down onto the concrete.

"What are you doing?" he yelled.

He couldn't have been more than twenty years old and only about five foot seven inches tall, and that's if I'm being generous. Without his ridiculous SUV, he was just a pansy-ass.

I held his neck hard. "I'm gonna spare your life, okay, but I'm gonna kick you in the stomach first and then I'm gonna go watch my baby be born." I stood up and kicked him right in the gut with only half the force I had in me.

"Have some manners, you little dickfuck!" I said and then turned and ran toward the entrance.

Tyler high-fived me on the way. When we got inside, I saw Jenny wheeling Mia through the giant double doors into the main hospital. Jenny moved out of the way for me to grab the handles of the wheelchair as we followed a nurse to the labor and delivery floor.

"We're going to take you into a triage room and check your vitals and cervix, and because your baby was breech, we'll do an ultrasound," the nurse said.

At that point, Mia was really out of it. I've never seen someone in so much pain in my life. Tyler and Jenny went off to the waiting room to call Mia's mom.

Once in the triage room, Mia stood up from the wheelchair and stripped off all her clothes. I put one of those wonky hospital gowns on her and then helped her up on the bed. Another contraction came right at that moment and splat! A gush of blood and water came out of her and onto the floor.

"Is that normal?"

"I don't know," she cried.

Having had a history of panicking in certain situations, I was amazed at how calm I was.

"Lie back, baby, you're doing so good." It must have been all those pregnancy books. I was nothing if not prepared.

The nurse arranged the table in front of the bed and then put a thick blue band around Mia's belly to monitor the baby's heartbeat. "Scoot your bottom down and spread your legs, honey." She reached down to check Mia's cervix while she simultaneously stared at the lines on the screen.

"You're at ten centimeters and fully effaced. I can feel the head. We need to get him out." She turned, picked up the phone, and mumbled something about fetal distress into the receiver.

"So his head is down?"

"Yes, he must have turned, but his heart rate is decreasing rapidly. We need to get him out. The doctor is on her way up from the second floor," the nurse said before continuing to prepare the room hurriedly.

The look on Mia's face was pure horror. My heart started racing and my hands went numb. When an alarm went off on the fetal monitor, Mia started crying. She was moaning and crying at the same time; it was so terrifying to see her losing it like that. All I could think of was that the baby was already two weeks early, and he was in distress, and my wife was lying there as scared as I was and in complete pain. Then it hit me, the thought that I could lose them both right there on that table. The fetal heart rate continued going down quickly. From the many books we'd read, Mia and I knew it was dangerously low. I squeezed her hand.

"Do something!" I yelled to the nurse.

Another nurse entered the room, still no Dr. Cho. I ran for a pair of latex gloves. I was going to deliver my baby, goddammit.

I looked over my shoulder and saw Mia grab the back of her legs. Yanking them toward her body, she began pushing on her own.

One nurse went to the end of the table while the other was preparing the baby station behind us. "That's good. Keep pushing," the nurse said.

"Are you going to catch him?" Mia could barely talk; she was practically hyperventilating.

"Of course I'm going to catch him, sweetheart." The nurse, who was preparing to catch our son, was a very petite woman.

Between Mia's legs, I could only see her from the shoulders up. Although I was relieved I wouldn't have to catch little Junior, I kept my latex gloves on just in case.

Martha entered the room, thank God. It should have been the doctor. I didn't know what was taking Dr. Cho so long, but I was happy Martha was there. I held one of Mia's legs back and Martha held the other so Mia could lean forward and push with everything she had.

With her other hand, Martha brushed the hair out of Mia's face, but she didn't say anything. The room was completely quiet except for the whimpering and mewling sounds Mia was making. At one point Mia screamed.

"His head is out," the nurse said.

From where we were standing, both Martha and I could see the baby's head. He was completely blue. I started to cry.

"One more push," Martha whispered to Mia in the gentlest voice I've ever heard.

I think I finally understood why Mia wanted her there so badly. I watched the nurse pull the umbilical cord off our baby's neck. It was wrapped so tightly that it left a large, red indentation on his new skin. It was one of the saddest moments of my life that I will never forget. I wondered how I would comfort Mia after such a tragedy. She would think it was her fault. Even though I'd watched her battle on, so selfless and determined to do the best by that baby, who would never get to thank her, Mia would blame herself for eternity. It's in those moments that you realize how brutal life can be. I told myself that I would have to be strong for her. That's what "through good times and bad" means.

Mia bent forward once more.

"Almost there, baby," I said to her as tears fell from my eyes and onto her cheeks.

She nodded but didn't make a sound as she pushed with the last bit of energy she had. Her face was red and covered in sweat. Martha released her leg, so I did the same. The moment our baby boy was out, they swooped him away to a plastic basinet under a bright light and monitor.

Mia crashed back down onto the table. "Go check him," she cried. That's all she was concerned about.

I hurried to the bassinet with the two nurses crowding him and now a neonatal doctor was also there.

The doctor was rubbing his body vigorously and saying, "Come on, little guy." She squeezed one puff of air from a ventilator into his mouth while a nurse was pricking the bottom of his foot, and then I heard his voice for the first time.

My first thought was thank you, Lord, Jesus Christ, Buddha, Mohammed, Infinite Spirit, Holy King, and all the rest, I will never use your name in vain again, thank you! And then, I'm not gonna lie, my next thought was my son can sing; he's got pipes, yes!

The moment he opened his eyes, he looked right at me and stopped crying on the spot. He cooed and I'm not one of those dads to brag or anything, but I swear to God he smiled—earliest smile on record.

They wrapped him up and handed my perfect child to me and said, "He's gonna be okay."

"Bring him over, Will," Martha said. She pulled Mia's gown down in front, exposing her breasts, and then she instructed me to unwrap him and put him on Mia's chest.

"Oh, oh, oh. Hi, baby," Mia said to the slimy little guy as she began to cry. All the pain and anxiety was gone. There she was, lying naked with her legs up in stirrups with our tiny, crying baby on her chest, and it was the most beautiful thing I've ever seen.

I bent and kissed her forehead. I couldn't stop the tears spilling from my eyes. "You did it. You were amazing. I love you so much." I sobbed.

"I love you too!" she said.

That's when Martha lost it. She hugged both of us over the bed. "Remember what I told you?" she said through tears.

"Yes. We have everything we need right here, between us," I replied.

Mia looked up at me, her eyes still full of tears. "We're a family now."

I kissed her lips softly. "Yes, baby."

Three years later . . .

Mia

W e're getting ready to go on the road. I'm excited to go cross-country with the boys. Oh, we've grown, by the way. Now Will and I have two sons, Allen and Dylan. They're three and two years old and they're maniacs, literally bouncing off the walls most days. Will says we should get them out to see the world, so we're going to play a few small venues here and there. We have a couple of band members going on the road with us, but mainly it's a family trip.

When we play music onstage, we give the boys either tambourines or shakers, and then we put big headphones on them so we don't damage their hearing. We try to play just loud enough to drown out any sounds they're making at the front. It's a lot of fun and they're learning. Will always says, "The family that plays together, stays together." I wouldn't have it any other way.

Will's neuroses calmed a great deal after the births of our boys. He had a few panicky moments, but once he settled into being a father, I knew he would be the best. He changed diapers and burped the babies for those many months in the early stages, and then when the boys got old enough to start on instruments, I saw Will truly light up. He'll sit at the piano with Allen or Dylan on his lap and sing along to the funny melodies they invent.

There are hard times, don't get me wrong, but I haven't forgotten what I learned so brutally a few years back when Will and I first met. I learned that you can't predict your future, there's no crystal ball or formula for happiness. You can't control the weather just like you can't control the way others behave, but what you can control is how much love you give. Surrendering to this crazy thing called life is hard, but we don't have to be the soulless sheets of paper tarrying along in the wind. We can find our people, love, respect them, and then hang on for dear life because it's not where you go on this journey but who you're with that matters the most.

Dear Reader,

Thank you so much for reading. I hope you enjoyed *Sweet Little Thing* and would consider sharing your thoughts by writing a review on the retailer website. Your feedback is greatly appreciated.

For the latest news, book details and other information visit my official website at www.reneecarlino.com or follow me on twitter @renayz.

Continue reading for a sneak peek at my upcoming novel
Nowhere But Here, releasing May 5, 2014
and available for pre-order NOW.

Excerpt from *Nowhere But Here*

I kicked my shoes off and rolled up my dress pants, then followed him to the edge of the pool where he set two towels down. He rolled up his jeans and sat gracefully before dunking his feet into the water. My fingers twitched with a desire to smooth back the disheveled hair that had fallen into his face. I watched intently as he reached up and ran his hand through it, displaying the flexing muscles in his arm. I couldn't take my eyes off him. When he handed my wine over, he noticed me staring.

"What?"

"Nothing." I shook my head. Looking down at my hands, I mumbled, "I just want to forget about everything for a little while."

"Really?" He looked excited when I nodded. "I have a great idea."

I dipped my feet in. The water was very warm, like bathwater. It instantly calmed my nerves.

"What's your idea?"

"Well, curious Katy, I'll show you."

He jumped up, ran to the gate, tinkered with something, and everything went off. The lights in the pool and all around the patio area, even the waterfall went off and it was silent. I could see steam pooling on the surface of the water. In the sky a million more stars became visible. I sipped my wine and then heard Will Ryan's soulful voice funneling softly through the outdoor speakers. Jamie appeared at my side.

"I love this guy. He's so good," I said.

"Yeah, he's awesome. He and his wife are playing at a little local bar on Saturday if you want to check it out with me?"

"I'd love to if I'm still here." I finally looked up and noticed that gorgeous Jamie was shirtless and undoing his belt buckle. Even in the dark I could see the sinewy muscles of his arms and his defined abs and chest. "What are you doing?" I whispered loudly, fighting to keep my voice low.

He smiled playfully. "We're gonna get your mind off things and take a little dip."

"I'm not!"

"No? Come on." He yanked his jeans off and leaped into the pool, wearing nothing but a pair of dark-blue-and-gray-plaid boxers."

When he surfaced, he held his boxers above his head, dangling on a single finger, and spun them around like he had done a striptease. He flung them toward me and they landed just to my left.

"Oh my god! I can't believe you just did that."

"What? You can't see me. Anyway, I know you have the crazy in you. You'll be in here in no time."

Sweet *Little* Thing

"Oh, how do you know that?"

"The pretty ones are always a little cray cray."

"You think you're so smart, don't you?"

"You have no idea," he said with no trace of humor. "Just get in here, Katy. I promise I won't look."

At that point, it's fair to say that I was drunk, completely and utterly drunk from the wine, and Jamie's presence was doing nothing to sober me up. His long, wet hair was leaving little glimmering droplets on his shoulders. I giggled. "Turn around, and you better not peek!"

"I promise."

He waded to one end of the pool and turned his back to me, at which point I quickly stripped down to my black bra and panties. Looking down, I thought they could easily pass for a swimsuit except that they were silk. *Oh well.*

As quietly as I could, I slipped into the pool on the opposite end of where Jamie stood. There was at least thirty yards between us. The pool felt amazing. I relaxed for a moment and then realized I was in a pool with a naked man I'd just met, a very attractive naked man.

"Okay, I'm in, Jamie, but keep a safe distance."

He turned around, grinned from ear to ear, and then disappeared under the water.

Good God, what is he doing?

I was suddenly very nervous; a small part of me was actually frightened. If it weren't for Will Ryan's sweet words pumping through the speakers, I would have been terrified. His hands on my hips didn't startle me at all because I could feel him getting closer. He rose out of the water, his warm hands gripping my waist. He wasn't smiling; he was searching my eyes. I looked around quickly and then back to his shoulders and rib cage as he lifted his arms and slicked his hair back with both hands. I could see his tensing neck muscles. There was very little stopping me from licking the drops of water off his arms. I closed my eyes as he closed the gap between us. I felt his mouth brush my neck and then move toward my ear. "Baby, open your eyes."

"I..."

"I know. You have a boyfriend." One side of his mouth turned up. He moved back a few inches. "We can be friends though, right?"

"Yes." I sighed.

"You were crying earlier. Why?'

I shook my head.

"Please tell me it wasn't because of how RJ treated you?"

"No."

"Then what?"

"Remember, I just want to forget everything."

He nodded, looking away for a second. "Are you ticklish?"

"Don't you dare."

He laughed. "Well there is one thing I know..."

"What's that, smart guy?"

He put his hands on my hips again and I let him, even though I knew it was crossing the line. It felt so good, like being enveloped by warmth and security.

His mouth turned up into a knowing smile, and then he said, almost wistfully, "Just friends is going to be hard, but I'll try. It's just that I like you. You're witty and sweet and you happen to be the most infinitely beautiful woman I've ever met."

I sucked in a startled breath. He paused, looking all drowsy with desire before opening his mouth to speak again.

"Don't," I murmured.

"It's not hyperbole, Katy. I promise."

Giggling nervously, I slowly sank beneath the water, thinking Jamie was out of his mind. I never would have described myself the way he had.

But then again, I had allowed Stephen to make me feel like I was barely worth coming home to . . .

Visit www.reneecarlino.com for
Nowhere But Here pre-order links.

Acknowledgments

I am grateful with all my heart for the unwavering support I've had from friends, family, readers, bloggers, and fellow authors. THANK YOU for reading *Sweet Thing* and writing about it and telling others about it long after the release. I don't know if I would have continued this story if it wasn't for your generous encouragement.

Getting back to Mia and Will was such a treat. They lived deep inside of my soul while I was away and that's where they'll go now, to live and love each other forever. Thank you for reading and being a part of this journey with me.

Chris Wojdak, thank you for bringing your talent to the project. I had so much fun watching you work. I'll be your assistant anytime!

Christina and Jhanteigh, you've both been great sounding boards on this and I appreciated your expertise through the process.

Gretchen de la O, A.L. Jackson, Emmy Montes, Toni Aleo, Julie Prestsater, Rebecca Shea and Hadley Quinn, what would I do without my weekly laugh with you girls? Thank you for being there when I needed a giant virtual hug.

Carey Heywood and Christina P, thank you for your helpful feedback and willingness to read at the drop of a hat.

And of course to the Rami's, for the many books worth of material you've given me and for happily being early draft readers.

Sarah Hansen, thank you for your great work, patience and for helping out during that small shit storm we had.

Zoe Norvell, thank you so much for sharing your talent with us.

Kim, Kylie, Joanna and Kim J, glad to have you girls to bounce things off of and to have a laugh with every now and then.

Anne Victory, thanks for working tirelessly and being flexible even though I'm always the last-minute girl.

A big thank you to Dawn Robinson for her support and for doing a fantastic job of last minute proofing.

Brandyn and Denyse, you made our dream cover a reality. You are not only stunning but professional and a joy to work with, thank you.

Ellie, you found us our Will. Need I say more? Thank you.

Katy Evans, thank you so much for your support and for reading the early draft. You've been such a great mentor to me.

Melanie, Brenda, Kaitlin, Sara, Kandace, Megan, Melanie, Cyndi, Stacey, Evangelina, and the babies, thank you for helping with the cover shoot and being a part of that fun day.

To my Ya Ya's: Heather, Katie, Angie, Rebecca, Carla and Noelle, thank you for the many years of inspiration and for nourishing a supportive group that values strength and leadership in women. Your encouragement has meant the world to me.

Heather, what would I do without you? You've been amazing and that isn't the half of it. Thank you for reading anything and everything I send you, even if I've written it in my sleep. You've been an awesome support, cheerleader, friend, and expert in this world. Love you and thank you.

To my boys, who are regularly subjected to my bizarre ideas and strange music choices, thank you for belting the songs out with me at the top of your lungs.

Anthony, it would be very hard for me to write a good hero if I didn't know at least one that existed in real life. Thanks for riding the wind with me.

CPSIA information can be obtained at www.ICGtesting.com
Printed in the USA
BVOW04s2207120514

353349BV00010B/140/P